I

A Time To Be (Re)Born

A Time To Be (Re)Born

A Biblical Journey
Through Lent

by
Rev. William F. Maestri

ALBA · HOUSE   NEW · YORK

SOCIETY OF ST. PAUL, 2187 VICTORY BLVD., STATEN ISLAND, NEW YORK 10314

Library of Congress Cataloging in Publication Data

Maestri, William.
  A time to be (re)born.

  1. Lenten sermons. 2. Catholic Church—Sermons.
  3.Sermons, American. 4. Bible—Homiletical use.
  I. Title.
  BV4277.M23   1982   252'.62   82-24336
  ISBN 0-8189-0447-X

Imprimatur:
†Stanley J. Ott, Vicar General
Auxiliary Bishop of New Orleans
July 15, 1982

Designed, printed and bound in the United States of
America by the Fathers and Brothers of the
Society of St. Paul, 2187 Victory Boulevard,
Staten Island, New York 10314, as part of their
communications apostolate.

---

2 3 4 5 6 7 8 9 (Current Printing: first digit)

Contents

A TIME TO BE (RE)BORN

Foreword

So much of the Bible is taken up with journeys and searches for the Lord. The father of all believers, Abraham, is given a new name and called to journey to a new land. Israel, God's own people, is constantly wandering and journeying in search of Yahweh and His will. In the New Testament, Jesus invites men and women to follow him and be part of the Kingdom. Paul, the great Apostle to the Gentiles, is a man familiar with journeying. On the road to Damascus he encounters the risen Lord, and begins his journey for life with Christ. The Bible is a witness to the fact that one's relationship with God is never static, nor can it be taken for granted. The Spirit blows where it wills. The disciple is the one who hears, sees and responds in faith to God's call to 'come and see' so as to be born anew.

Our own lives, often less dramatic than those of the figures encountered in Scripture, nonetheless are caught up in a faith-journey toward God. Each day we are challenged to see, hear and respond to His presence in our often noisy and cluttered world. Lent is an excellent time to pause and rethink our relationship with God and those around us. Lent is a time to re-examine those forgotten areas of our life that have gathered dust through neglect. Simply put: Lent is the acceptable time for us to reawaken a sense of God's Spirit in our hearts and everyday relationships. The Christian life is a journey in faith that travels through everyday existence. The Christian accepts each day as the setting for encountering God and His call to conversion and new life. The Christian is on a journey and a search for God. This journey does not avoid everyday life but travels deep into each moment.

It is with the conviction that our faith-life is one of journeying toward God, that these biblical reflections are offered. What follows is a brief Scriptural summary of the daily readings for Lent, and a reflection on the readings. These reflections are not meant to be a substitute for one's own Lenten journey into the Lord. Rather, it is hoped that such a summary and reflection will aid the homilist and the general reader in his or her own personal search for God who makes all things new.

A special word of thanks is extended to the Monks of St. Joseph Abbey and Abbot David Melancon, O.S.B., to whom this book is dedicated. Such good friends in faith are signals that the God we seek has already found us. Also I would like to thank Rev. Timothy Chenevey and the Society of St. Paul for allowing me to express part of my journey in faith. I would like to express my gratitude to Patricia Kives and Paul Worm for cheerfully typing the manuscript.

Rev. William F. Maestri
St. Joseph Seminary College
St. Benedict, La.

To see Thee in the end and the beginning;
Thou carriest us and Thou dost go before;
Thou art the journey and the journey's end.

King Alfred

The Journey Begins

Ash Wednesday
Joel 2:12-18
2 Corinthians 5:20—6:2
Matthew 6:1-6, 16-18

The prophet Joel announces the day of the Lord and calls for conversion by all the people. The people can no longer conduct their lives as usual, for the Lord is near. A sense of urgency is present. Hence the trumpet is to be sounded, the community gathers, and even the responsibilities of the newly married are to give way to preparing for the Lord. True preparation calls for one to have a change of heart and not just of the outer appearance. Finally, Joel reminds the community that God is gracious, merciful, and filled with kindness.

The depth of God's love and graciousness is revealed in the gift of Jesus. St. Paul in his letter to the Corinthians reminds them that in Christ sin has been overcome. Each person is called to personal holiness in imitation of God. Again the theme of urgency is stressed. Now is the acceptable time of salvation. God is working through us each day of our lives.

In the Gospel, Jesus continues the call for conversion and a change of heart. Jesus reminds the disciples that external forms of piety (almsgiving, prayer and fasting) are not enough. One must experience an inward change. External piety is always a means for growing in love of God and personal holiness. All of our good works are to be directed to the Father who alone is good.

THE ACCEPTABLE TIME

In the Broadway musical, *The Music Man*, Professor Harold Hill tells Marian that if she puts off until tomorrow what is required today, she will collect a large number of empty yesterdays. Professor Hill was teaching the truth of the acceptable time. Lent is the call to respond to God's acceptable time for us. Lent comes from a word that means 'spring.' Spring is the time of new beginnings, rebirth and the bursting forth of life. Spring is the season of hope that tells us death does not have the last word. Life is stronger than death, and the darkness of winter must give way to the light and life of spring. Spring is nature's refusal to collect empty yesterdays.

Lent is the acceptable time for us to call a halt to life as usual. The Church is asking us to reexamine our relationship with God and one another. We are being asked to re-evaluate the things that really matter: God, human relationships and the quality of our faith life. Lent is the acceptable time of conversion and change of heart. The prophet Joel reminds us that it is not enough to change our outward appearance, but that real conversion takes place at the level of our spirit responding to God's Holy Spirit. Sackcloth and ashes are only physical expressions of what is taking place in the depth of our being. Jesus clearly reminds us that all of our good works are to be done so that God the Father may be praised. Piety is growth in God's holiness and never the seeking after human praise.

The prophet Joel and the apostle Paul speak to us with a sense of urgency. Even *now* the Lord is calling us to return to Him with our whole heart. *Now* is the time of God's healing presence. Yesterday is but a memory and tomorrow is only a promise. This kind and gracious God has given us today as the acceptable time. Today is the time to open our hearts, respond in faith, and be healed. Lent and spring are ultimately seasons of life and hope. They speak to us of the great mystery of Jesus. It is through the cross that the glory of the resurrection is made visible. It is in dying that one is born to eternal life. Such dying and rising, and their message of hope, are not for tomorrow but for today. Such a message is for each of us!

Thursday after Ash Wednesday
Deuteronomy 30:15-20
Luke 9:22-25

In our first reading, Moses places before the Israelites the ultimate choice: life and prosperity, death and doom. The way of life is the way of obedience to the Lord's commands. Such obedience is the great act of love toward God. The Lord will never be outdone in generosity. For all who obey in love, God will bestow countless blessings. However, the Israelites are free to reject God and His commands. They can worship false gods and choose destruction. Idols can never give life; they only take it and in the end disappoint. Only the Lord is rich in kindness, mercy and life.

Jesus continues the theme of choosing life or death. The true disciple is one who follows Jesus through the cross. The cross takes many forms: suffering, rejection, death and self-denial. Yet the cross leads to resurrection. However, we can choose the way of the world and seek to gain all its riches. But in the end we have lost everything. The call to decide for life or death must be done each day.

LIFE THROUGH DEATH

How strange today's readings sound to the modern ear. Moses tells us that life and prosperity come to those who are obedient to God's will. Obedience in fact is the great proof of love and reverence. Only the mature and truly free person can obediently submit to the will of another or to God. The immature and self-indulgent person must always be doing his own thing. The immature person confuses license with liberty. Every truly free and loving act demands a decision to limit and commit oneself. God, out of love, committed Himself to a given people. In the greatest proof of His love, God became human in Jesus. God forever committed Himself to our human condition and history. Through this free, loving act of Divine giving, we have the hope of resurrection. The same is true for each of us. For example, husband and wife say yes to each other in a faithful, exclusive way. They witness to love and freedom by a decision to be for the other.

In our Gospel, Jesus indicates the cost of true love, obedience and fidelity to the Father's will. Jesus will be baptized with the fire of the cross. But not only Jesus; all who choose to follow him must drink the same cup and carry the same cross. Granted, few of us may be physically nailed to a cross. Our personal crosses are often more subtle and hidden, but no less real. We often struggle with the cross of pride, egoism, self-centeredness and a blindness to God's presence in our lives. Our cross is the struggle to be for God and others as much as we are for ourselves. Our cup is the struggle to see the richness of God poured into our hearts. Too often we spend our life trying to save it by the standards of the world. We seek security and meaning in the bread and trophies which rust destroys and thieves break in and steal. Jesus is telling us that God alone is our hope and strength. God's love for us endures forever. Only in dying to all that is not God do we have the hope of eternal life.

Finally, Jesus is reminding us that true life is a gift and a call to journey in search of God. This journey is never easy. We are not excused from life. On the contrary, we are called each day to take up our cross and follow in the steps of the One who showed us the way. Let us pray for the courage to choose life in God!

Friday after Ash Wednesday
Isaiah 58:1-9
Matthew 9:14-15

The prophet Isaiah indicates that it is never enough to fast and perform external works of mortification. Yahweh is a God of justice who acts on behalf of the lowly. A true seeking after the Lord comes to those who do justice through love. The Lord comes to those who set the oppressed free; share with the needy; make welcome the homeless; and care for all the needs of one's neighbor. Only then will God respond to our call. Only after we have been a people committed to justice and love can we hope to find God. God is present in the outcast. It is through solidarity with the poor that God cries out: Here I Am! In our gospel readings, Jesus is not rejecting fasting and penance. However, Jesus comes to announce the Kingdom, and so we must rejoice and celebrate. Yet there is a time for fasting. The shadow of the cross is present even as Jesus speaks. For there will be a day when the groom is taken away. But for now rejoice.

LENTEN PRUDENCE

The Greek philosopher Aristotle and the Catholic saint Thomas Aquinas wrote about the virtues of prudence and temperance. Prudence is the ability to practice good judgment in every situation. Prudence is the virtue of uncommon common sense. Temperance is the moral virtue which helps us to keep our balance. The temperate person avoids too much or too little. Putting these two virtues together, we arrive at a disposition of the soul in which we exercise good judgment by avoiding extremes. In the words of St. Thomas, virtue dwells in the middle. Balance and common sense are good advice in the season of Lent.

Isaiah and Jesus are calling us to live a life of balance and common sense. Isaiah reminds us that piety and faith are never private affairs between us and God. There is a social dimension to faith because there is a social dimension to human existence. It is not good for us to be alone. Our vertical relationship with God can never be separated from our horizontal relationships with others. We are called to love God and our neighbor as much as we love ourselves. We cannot be saved by ourselves apart from the community of faith. Isaiah reminds us that if we truly are searching for God, we need look no further than there in the enslaved, the hungry, the oppressed and homeless, the naked and all who are lacking in basic necessities. Isaiah is challenging us to reach for a balanced spirituality between personal holiness and concern for the needs of others. There is no real separation between the two. Faith without works is dead, and works without faith is pride. In our Lenten search for God, we are inevitably introduced to our neighbor.

Jesus appeals to our common sense. "How can wedding guests go in mourning so long as the groom is with them?" The answer is obvious: they can't. At a wedding we celebrate and rejoice. The person and ministry of Jesus are the source of Christian joy. This does not mean that we reject fasting and mourning as inappropriate. Rather, Jesus is calling us to be prudent and to know when and how to express both joy and sorrow. The Book of Ecclesiastes tells us that there is "a time for tears, a time for laughter; a time for mourning, a time for dancing."

Our Lenten program for spiritually growing in the Lord needs the balance of Isaiah and the common sense of Jesus. Lent is a time to grow in personal holiness and sensitivity to the needs of others. Lent is more than giving up our favorite food.

Lent is growing up into the full measure of God's people with grace, and spirit and truth.

Saturday after Ash Wednesday
Isaiah 58:9-14
Luke 5:27-32

Isaiah continues to remind the Israelites of what is required of those who search for God and His ways. Yahweh is a God of liberation, and all forms of oppression are out of order. To seek the Lord in spirit and truth means one must be a person who is free from anger, lies and an uncontrolled tongue. The person who does the will of the Lord is generous and responds to the needs of the lowly. In so doing, our darkness becomes light; the parched land is made fruitful; and all forms of brokenness are healed. However, this calls for one to be open to the Lord and His ways. Only then will our strength be renewed.

Jesus continues to announce the good news of salvation and freedom. Jesus calls a tax collector (Matthew-Levi) and even goes to his house for a dinner with other folk of ill repute. The self-righteous Pharisees and scribes are shocked. Jesus should not associate with such types. Yet Jesus reminds them that is why he came: "I have come to invite sinners to a change of heart." The healthy and self-righteous have no need of the Divine Physician.

FOLLOW ME

We can only imagine what must have gone on in the mind of Matthew on the day of his rebirth. No doubt it was business as usual. The tax collector, hated by the Jews for being an agent of Rome, was exacting his pound of flesh. In the routine of his everyday life, Jesus comes and challenges him to begin again. Jesus is calling Matthew to a journey in faith. Yet how strange! Tax collectors and sinners were birds of a feather. What could Jesus possibly see in them? What could they possibly do for Jesus? The answer is simple: nothing and everything. It is true they had nothing to offer. Their standing in the community was one of suspicion by the Romans and hatred by the Jews. Yet Jesus saw possibilities in every person. Since each person is a child of God, no one is beyond dignity and respect. Maybe for the first time, someone recognized the possibilities in Matthew, and he responded with his whole heart. All we know for sure is that life was never the same after the call of Jesus to follow him.

Our own personal journey in faith can be much the same. At times we can often feel the judgment of others and our own self-rejection. We can experience the negative effects of guilt, which keep us chained to the past and closed to the future. It is in the middle of such situations that Jesus comes and says, "Follow me." Again, it is not because we are righteous, perfect or healthy. Jesus does not invite us to fellowship with him because we have earned such a call. Rather, Jesus comes as the Father's true gift to all who are in need of a change of heart. Maybe we don't feel worthy of responding. Maybe we feel hypocritical and insincere in coming to Jesus with our concerns. The story of Matthew offers us courage. It says simply to leave all such fears aside and trust in the One who is always faithful to His word. We can surrender our anxieties and uncertainties to the One who knows what we need before we even ask.

For those of us who have been lukewarm toward Jesus, and for those who have traveled to a distant land, the words of Jesus speak to our heart: "Follow me. Come after me and experience the healing love and acceptance of my Father and your Father. Come and be forgiven and nourished at my table with the food that never perishes. Come as you are, but come and experience what life is meant to be." These are bold words, but we can believe them. For in the words of Isaiah, "light shall rise for you in the darkness, and the gloom shall become for you like midday; then the Lord will guide you always . . . He will renew your strength."

First Week of Lent

Monday of the First Week
Leviticus 19:1-2, 11-18
Matthew 25:31-46

The book of Leviticus is the book of Holiness.
Yahweh tells Moses that He is the very essence of
holiness, and expects His people to be holy as well.
How? By loving the Lord and entering into right relationships with others. Holiness calls for us to reverence
the Lord's name and stand in awe of all He has done.
Beyond that, holiness calls us to deal justly with our
neighbor. We are not to steal, lie, curse, or utter dishonest judgments. No one is to seek revenge. In a single
command: the essence of holiness is to love the neighbor as we love ourselves. In so doing we acknowledge
the holiness of the Lord.

Matthew's Gospel presents the great eschatological
scene of judgment at the end of the world. Those who
will enter eternal life are the ones who responded to the
needs of their neighbor. Eternal punishment is reserved
for those who fail to meet the minimum requirements
of God's Kingdom. It is in the least of our brothers and
sisters that we minister to Jesus in his needs.

THE HIDDENNESS OF GOD

Much of our journey for God is dependent on the ability
to see. Sight is not limited to the eye, but involves the
heart—our whole being. To see means to be sensitive and
attentive to the richness of everyday life. True sight is the
discipline to look beyond the surface and grasp the meaning
of experiences, events and persons. Such vision is not easy
today. Our everyday world is such that reality is one-

dimensional—the physical. Only that which can be measured, quantified and expressed scientifically is treated as real. We find it difficult to move beyond the senses to the level of the Spirit. The everyday in which we live seems so present with all that is not divine, sacred and holy. The newspaper and television highlight so much of what is inhuman and anti-Spirit. At the other end of the spectrum, we can be filled with pride at technological and scientific achievements which give the illusion that we are self-sufficient.

For the person who is honestly searching for God, what can we say? Few of us are swept up into the heights of spiritual ecstasy. We are called to find God in the 'dapple things of life.' God is not indifferent, but is passionately in love with us. Often we are blinded by our everyday life filled with so much banality, routine, boredom and fatigue. Yet it is in the everydayness of our life that God is at work luring us to greater levels of love and sensitivity. In the midst of our everyday, God is working quiet miracles and making straight the rough roads. In the words of Father Teilhard, our everyday world is filled with 'the presence of God as the atmosphere in which we are bathed.'

The ability to discern the hidden presence of God is no small matter. Our readings from Leviticus and the Gospel of Matthew indicate how important it is to find God. Both readings tell us that our search for God must always involve a search for our neighbor. Holiness demands that we treat others with dignity and respect. Because the God we seek is Holy, we are to be holy and just toward others. Jesus goes so far as to say that he is present in the hungry, thirsty, homeless, naked, ill and imprisoned. Eternal life is offered to those who responded in love to neighbors in need. Eternal punishment awaits those who failed to see Jesus in another human being.

Lent is the season for getting our hearts in focus. It is the time for us to search for the God who lives in unapproachable light, yet also dwells in the needy neighbor. God lives deep within the heart of each of us.

Tuesday of the First Week
Isaiah 55:10-11
Matthew 6:7-15

The power of the prophet is the authority of the Lord's word being proclaimed through him. Isaiah reminds us that the word of the Lord is a gift, and never returns without doing its work. The word of the Lord is a gift as much as the rain, the snow and the fruitful earth. The Lord not only nourishes our physical needs, He also provides for our spiritual hungers through the word.

The One to whom we pray is our good Father who knows what we need before we ask Him. We do not need to say a great deal. God knows us so well that the hairs of our head are counted. The Lord requires of us a forgiving spirit. All forms of our piety are acceptable only if we are at peace with our brothers and sisters. God has forgiven us in Jesus, and we are to forgive one another.

PRAYER: LESS IS MORE

In the Rule of St. Benedict we find the following: "The wise man is known by the fewness of his words." Our Gospel reading would also say, so is the person of prayer. Jesus tells the disciples that they need not "storm heaven" in order to receive what they truly need. God knows what is required before we ever ask. In effect, Jesus is saying that basic trust is required in our relationship with God. Such trust is expected, since God is really our loving Parent who wants what is best for us. Jesus clearly indicates that prayer, before it is petition, is recognition. Prayer is an awareness of whom we address, namely, the kind and merciful Lord who sends rain and snow so the earth will be fertile and fruitful. The God to whom we pray is the gracious Giver of good gifts to all people. The greatest gift is Jesus the only Son.

Once we recognize that God is our Father, we can in confidence ask to receive what we truly need: reverence for God's name; the realization of His Kingdom in our lives; our daily bread; protection from evil; and the willingness to forgive others as we have been forgiven. All these needs speak to us of the necessity of living in God's presence each day. Prayer never becomes a shopping list of our wants, but an open heart to humbly receive what God wants to give us.

Yet in our daily prayer life we often feel the compulsion to 'rattle on like the pagan.' Why? Perhaps we relate to God like we do to our parents or authority figures. They only respond if we keep the pressure on. Perhaps it is our basic insecurity which does not allow us to trust in God's loving care. If we don't continually let God know we are in need, He might forget us. But perhaps more to the point, if we are constantly speaking it is almost impossible to listen. If we don't listen to what God wants of us, we can always say we didn't know. Hence, we are excused and not responsible. It is much easier to speak and let God know what we want. Yet, prayer can never be effectively experienced without silence. We need to be alone with God, and just listen to the Spirit speak to our spirit. We need to be attuned to what the Lord requires, and be willing to respond. In our often loud and hectic world, listening and silence are in short supply. Yet these are required if we are to pray in imitation of Jesus.

Lent is usually the season when we try to 'pray more.' St. Paul calls us to pray unceasingly. Yet we need to be clear as to what Jesus means by prayer. It is not the multiplication of words or empty phrases. Rather, true prayer is best disclosed by Mary and Jesus. At the Annunciation, Mary indicates that she is the servant of the Lord and His will shall be done through her. Jesus in the Garden of Gethsemane prays that the Father's will be done always. True prayer is short on words but deep in trust in the God who is our Father.

Wednesday of the First Week
Jonah 3:1-10
Luke 11:29-32

The Lord raises up Jonah and gives him the mission to proclaim God's word of judgment. Jonah proclaims this word, and to his surprise and disappointment, the Ninevites repent. Even the king puts on the sackcloth and ashes. Everyone is to turn from evil and ask the Lord for forgiveness and healing. The Lord sees how sincere the people are, and he does not bring about their destruction. We know that Jonah did not approve of God's mercy.

In our Gospel, the crowd wants a sign so that they can believe in Jesus. Jesus says the only sign given is that of Jonah. When Jonah preached the people turned to God. Jesus is greater than Jonah for he is the Son of Man. The Son of Man is Jesus' favorite title (used 82 times in the Gospels). In the Old Testament the Son of Man appears only once (Dn 7:13), as the eschatological figure who comes to judge and announce God's rule. Jesus, as the Son of Man, comes to announce the Kingdom and calls for all people to repent and reform their lives. Unlike Jonah, Jesus is rejected and will be put to death, only to rise in three days.

THE GOD PROBLEM

In the 1960's, a theological movement began called 'the Death of God' school. Basically this movement taught that modern man could no longer believe in God or a transcendent reality. Science, evil, modern philosophy and outdated theologies all worked against belief in God. There developed a number of books and courses concerned with the so-called 'God problem.' The last two decades have witnessed the death of the God theologies. In fact, there has been a spiritual revival of sorts in America (conservative-Pentecostal churches) and throughout the world (Islamic fundamentalism). Both Jonah and the crowd in our Gospel have a God problem. Not the one of modern man, but a problem in understanding God and His ways.

Jonah expresses no hesitation in being a prophet as long as he is a prophet of doom and gloom. He will gladly announce the Lord's wrath and judgment. The great city Nineveh will finally get what it deserves. The Lord is just and in His justice He will destroy this great city. However, Jonah has a God problem. Jonah finds out that God's justice and mercy cannot be separated. The Lord does not desire death and destruction. Rather the Lord wants all people to experience a change of heart and be converted. This is too much for Jonah. He fails to realize that justice without mercy is cruelty.

The crowd which pressed around Jesus has a God problem as well. The Messiah should be a figure of great pomp, power and worldly fame. The Messiah is God's savior who should come to call the righteous. However, Jesus fits none of these expectations. Jesus, the Son of Man, is born in a stable. He is the Son of Mary and the carpenter Joseph. He associates with all the wrong people: sinners, tax collectors, Samaritans and women of ill repute. In fact, he even eats with them and says they are called to places of honor in the Kingdom. The full scandal of Jesus is present on the cross. The One who comes announcing good news: "the blind see; the lame walk; and the poor have the gospel preached to them"—is laid in a borrowed tomb. Yet in Jesus there is something greater than Solomon and Jonah. The cross and the empty tomb speak to us of the power of God to save all who believe.

In our Lenten journey toward God, it is helpful to examine our own God problem. Is our God too small, so as to allow no room for justice *and* mercy? Is our God too predictable, so as to allow no room for surprises and the doing of new things? If so, this is not the God of Abraham, Isaac, Jacob and Jesus. The God of the Bible is the dynamic Lord who makes all things new, and challenges us to be part of His great adventure.

Thursday of the First Week
Esther 14:3-19 (NAB, C:14-30)
Matthew 7:7-12

Esther is a woman of great faith and courage. She is a Jew and also the queen of Persia. Her husband King Ahasuerus is determined to kill all the Jews. However, Esther, in great anguish, lifts up her voice to the Lord. She believes that Yahweh is a faithful God who will not leave His people in time of trouble. Esther reminds the Lord how special Israel is to Him. As the mighty hand of Yahweh saved Israel from Pharaoh, so now the Lord must come to the rescue of His people. Esther's only hope is in the Lord. Yahweh responds and saves Israel.

The notion of a faithful God is continued by Jesus. He uses the analogy of earthly parents to explain our relationship with God the Father. Parents who truly love their children provide for their true needs. The love of the Father for each of us is similar: though infinitely greater, God responds to our asking, seeking and knocking. What God requires of us is trust and the willingness to love as He loves us. If we truly love and trust God and serve our neighbors, then we become people of the Kingdom.

A RESTFUL HEART

St. Augustine, in his spiritual autobiography, *The Confessions*, writes that we are restless until we rest in God. Augustine surely knew of what he wrote. Much of his life was a journeying after that which would give him peace. Augustine searched for peace in philosophy, worldly fame and the life of pleasure. However, all of these left him empty. All the while his mother, Monica, prayed for his conversion. Finally, he met the great bishop Ambrose. Augustine was baptized and became a great bishop and teacher. More importantly, he joined Monica and Ambrose in sainthood. They all knew that true peace only comes to those who rest in the Lord. This journey toward God is seldom straight and without detours. Yet the Spirit works mightily to light our way. The restlessness of our hearts will be quieted only when we open our hearts to the Spirit.

Our readings speak of distress and the restless heart. Queen Esther was at the limit of her earthly resources. Only the Lord could bring deliverance. Esther was mindful that the Lord is a faithful God who never goes back on His covenant of love. As Israel was delivered from bondage in Egypt, Esther prays that her people will be delivered from King Ahasuerus. In her lowliness and powerlessness, the strength of the Lord reaches perfection. In the words of our responsorial psalm, "Lord, on the day I called for help, you answered me." Esther is reminding us that true courage and security come only from the Lord who knows all things.

In the Gospel our restless hearts find a home in the words of Jesus. Jesus tells us that God is not indifferent to our needs, but is ready to meet our daily concerns. All we need do is ask, search, knock, and treat others the way we want to be treated. We are to *ask* that God's will be done through us each day. We are to seek after the Lord in all our daily works. The door of our heart is to be *opened* so that the Spirit can transform our heart of stone into flesh. The words of Jesus are spoken to our restless heart in its doubts, confusion, lostness and uncertainty. Jesus is clearly challenging us to seek after the Lord and turn away from sin. True happiness and peace never come to those who worship the idols of materialism, popularity and worldly power. The restful heart comes as a gift to those who treat friends as friends and turn the enemy into a neighbor. The Father will never be outdone in generosity and love.

Lent is a time to join Esther, the disciples, Augustine, Ambrose and Monica in search for God and rebirth in the Spirit. Lent is the season to ask, search, knock and love. Let us examine the restlessness of our lives and see where we have excluded God. Let us reflect on the ways in which we have trusted the wisdom of the world, and too little in the Lord who knows all things. We need not fear. The love of God drives out all fear. Do not be anxious. Our God is a loving Father who gives all that is required for a restful heart.

Friday of the First Week
Ezekiel 18:21-28
Matthew 5:20-26

Ezekiel is the Lord's prophet during the Babylonian exile (586 B.C.). The Exile is a low point in Israel's history, and a low point in the covenant relationship with Yahweh. Ezekiel reminds the people of the need to obey the covenant. After all, the Lord does not desire anyone to be lost. Rather, the Lord rejoices when one turns from evil to do good. However, God's justice requires that each person be treated according to his deeds. To live apart from God brings exile and death. To those who turn from sin and obey the Lord a long life will be given.

The words of Jesus complete the process of turning to the Lord. For not only must our behavior or deeds be pleasing to God, but also our intentions. True conversion is an inward change of heart which affects the way we act. It is not enough to refrain from murder; one must overcome the inner feelings of bitterness and hatred which cause violence and death. Jesus is not rejecting the need for liturgical worship. However, to bring gifts to the altar without being at peace with others is incomplete. True worship requires that we be reconciled with God and our neighbors.

RECONCILIATION

The seasons of Advent and Lent blend to remind us of an essential insight into the Christian story: new life does not come without suffering. Love is never free, but always calls for a willingness on our part to be poured out on behalf of others. We know this because Jesus' birth, ministry and death came at a dear price. The birth of Jesus, like every birth, began with the shedding of blood and the cry of pain. The ministry of Jesus knew a great deal of hostility and rejection. The shedding of blood at birth becomes a full pouring out on the Cross. Jesus loves to the end, the utmost, and invites us to do the same. The reconciliation between God and humankind was not achieved without suffering and the shedding of blood. We cannot have a true reconciliation without the willingness to die to the old self so as to be born anew. It is only by daily dying to self through the Cross that we grow into Christ.

Ezekiel reminds the Israelites, who are in exile, that they must change their ways. The reason they are under Babylonian domination is because they have abandoned the covenant and sinned. Only if they are willing to repent and begin again is there hope. If not, they will only sink deeper into alienation and death. However, change is never easy. We fall into patterns and life styles which become comfortable and predictable. We take things and relationships for granted. We become insensitive to God and others. Yet God is always ready to welcome us home. God stands ready, and actively seeks us in reconciliation. We must do our part. We must be willing to change and grow. We must be willing to give up the old securities, turn from sin, and be reborn.

Reconciliation and conversion never stop at the surface of external behavior. Jesus indicates that true reconciliation and conversion demand a change of attitude, feelings, values, and the way in which we see the world. The Scribes and Pharisees may have performed correct actions, but their hearts were untouched. They wanted holiness and a right relationship with God without sacrifice or cost. They wanted cheap grace! Jesus clearly says that true discipleship must extend beyond offering gifts on the altar, seeking earthly justice in courts, and refraining from physical murder. True Christian living flows from Christian attitudes and values. The Christian is one who refrains from those promiscuous inner feelings which stifle the Spirit. We must be healed in our hearts of anger, envy, jealousy and vengeance.

Lent is the time for such a healing and rebirth. Lent is the season for putting on Christ and being reconciled with God. Once we have been healed in our hearts, we can reach out to others in freedom, love and peace. The reconciling joy of Jesus will be ours.

Saturday of the First Week
Deuteronomy 26:16-19
Matthew 5:43-48

The main concern of the Bible is the covenant relationship between God and humankind in history. God freely enters into relationship with people, the Israelites, and offers the hope for lasting liberation from sin and death. The Book of Deuteronomy, the Book of the Second Law, is the account of the covenant between Yahweh and His people. Under Moses' leadership the people are to obey the commands of the Lord and listen to His voice. The Israelites are God's own, and are called to be faithful to the covenant.

Jesus comes to perfect the Law and bring it to completion. He does this through the command to love— not in an abstract way, but to love the person who needs us now. This even means that we must love the enemy. If we only love those who return our love we have done little. We are to pray for those who hurt us. We are to avoid judgments about others. The gifts of rain and sun are given to both the good and the bad. We are to be perfect in imitation of the Father.

BE PERFECT

The English writer G.K. Chesterton once remarked that Christianity was not rejected because it was found wanting, but tried and found too hard. Those insightful and sobering words add much realism to our often watered-down Christianity. The words of Chesterton remind us that to follow Christ is to embrace the way of life that demands commitment not comfort. So much of our everyday life and religion is comfort-oriented. We are surrounded by convenience appliances and instant work savers. Much of our religion has become comfort-centered: air-conditioned churches, vigil Masses, and comfortable kneelers. This can easily lead us into the illusion that following Jesus is possible without self-denial and the cross. The most serious challenge to the Christian witness is sentimentality. We can come to believe that following Jesus is a way of the emotions rather than a decision of the will. Sentiment is the way of comfort. Discipleship requires commitment.

Moses tells the Israelites that their covenant relationship with Yahweh is no trivial matter. It will require hard work and effort. They must be careful in obeying the Law and walk in His ways. The Israelites are God's very special people and much will be required of them. Their election and the covenant are not reasons to boast. Rather, they indicate how much God will require of His people.

Jesus brings into clear focus just how much is demanded of the Christian. We cannot be satisfied to love our family, countrymen, fellow believers, and those who love us. Rather, the Christian is challenged to love and pray for the enemy. We are to do good to the one who tries to make life uncomfortable for us. The Christian cannot be satisfied with a humanistic ethic that says 'live and let live,' and 'treat others the way they treat you.' The Christian can never resort to violence, hatred and evil. Only love and prayer have the power to transform the brokenness of life into a peaceful harmony.

Who can do this? Who can really love the enemy? At times we have trouble loving our friends. Remember the words of Chesterton—tried and found too hard. Yet the words of Jesus are clear: "You must be made perfect as your heavenly Father is perfect." How do we achieve this? Simple: we don't. The Christian life is not an achievement but a gift from our good and gracious God. Growth in the Christian life comes to those who realize that human potential is quite limited. Christian realism indicates how much we are in need of God's Spirit. It is in our weakness and inadequacy that the challenge comes: love your enemies and pray for them; be perfect as your heavenly Father. This is not done to frustrate us, but to indicate what is possible when God is allowed to work in our hearts.

To live in imitation of Jesus is the main journey of the Christian life. Such a journey does not allow for the sentiment of comfort. It demands a willingness to be committed to the person of Jesus and the Cross. Jesus demands a great deal—be perfect! Be confident, for Jesus has showed us the way.

Second Week of Lent

Monday of the Second Week
Daniel 9:4-10
Luke 6:36-38

The prophet Daniel reminds the Israelites that it is not enough for individuals to have a change of heart; the whole nation must be converted to the Lord. There is a corporate or social dimension to sin and injustice. Hence, there is also a corporate need for conversion and repentance. Daniel throughout this passage uses the collective 'we' to indicate that individual actions have effects on the community. Yet Daniel also offers hope by calling God compassionate and forgiving. However, the whole nation must return to the covenant.

The theme of God's compassion is stressed by Jesus in the Gospel. The disciple of Jesus is to refrain from judging, condemning, and being hard of heart. Rather, those who follow Jesus are to be compassionate, forgiving and generous, and give to others as they have received. Why? Simply because God expects us to treat others the way we have been treated. In so doing we will give praise to the Father.

Both Daniel and Jesus remind us that an essential part of conversion is compassion. In our individual relationships and institutional structures, justice and compassion are required.

BE COMPASSIONATE

One of America's leading insurance companies uses the slogan, "there is no one exactly like you." A manufacturer of women's perfume says its product produces a different scent for each woman who wears it. We can have our hamburgers individually made to our own taste. Clothes, cars and various other products are sold promising to enhance our individuality. We are as unique as our fingerprints, and Madison Avenue has mass produced the desire to be different! However, such uniqueness and individuality do not come without consequences to other dimensions of life. Namely, if we are so unique and different then a sense of loneliness becomes acute. If there is no one like me, then it becomes impossible to share significant moments and experiences. The other will never be able to relate to my hopes and dreams, pains and pleasures, disappointments and achievements. Such loneliness and isolation become a solitary confinement from which there is no relief. To be too unique and too much of an individual is to be imprisoned in one's own universe. We can never transcend our feelings, values and worldview. Simply put, we can never love the other since we can never really know the other. The consequences of such isolation are all too common. The levels of indifference and violence that are part of our everyday world witness to the negative effects of an exaggerated and false uniqueness.

The need to be compassionate is crucial for our Christian and civic life. Compassion does not recognize so much that which divides us, as that which unites us. Namely, compassion recognizes that beneath the differences of age, color, sex, class, religion and nationality we are the loving handiwork of God. Each person is made in the image and likeness of God. Because of our common authorship, each person is due respect and dignity. Compassion is the challenge to see beyond the externals, and celebrate that which binds us into a common human family. Only when compassion is at work in our hearts can we have the courage to pardon, refrain from harsh judgments, and be generous with the other. Only when compassion is present can we see the other as brother or sister. The prophet Daniel reminds us that compassion must have a corporate dimension. We need to be a church, community and society which seeks after justice and compassion.

Jesus' challenge to be compassionate is not a call for a blind uniformity. The gracious God who called us into existence has given each of us gifts and talents. However, these are to be used for the common good. Gifts are not meant to be buried, or used as a form of control or power. Gifts from God are given so that the Father will be praised. Each of us has a work to do in helping to build God's Kingdom. Yet, laboring for the Lord always requires a sense of solidarity and oneness with others. Compassion opens our eyes and liberates our hearts, to see how much we share in common. Most especially, we are a family of the God who is forgiving and compassionate.

Tuesday of the Second Week
Isaiah 1:10, 16-20
Matthew 23:1-12

The prophetic word is never ambiguous. If the nations refuse to give up evil and follow the Lord, destruction will follow. On the other hand, Yahweh is always ready to forgive and renew the covenant. Isaiah is crystal clear in his message: give up the sins of injustice and evil. Set things right and seek after God's justice. Only when misdeeds are rejected, and the people listen to God's word will healing come. If not, death is certain.

The real prophets and teachers are those who do more than proclaim the word of the Lord; they live it. The Pharisees and Scribes follow Moses, but they fail to live what they require of others. They are moralistic and legalistic. They love the titles of honor such as 'teacher' and seek places of honor in public. They exalt themselves and proclaim their self-importance. Yet Jesus reminds us that the way of discipleship is through humility and service.

Humility calls us to acknowledge our sins and ask for the Lord's healing. We need not fear. Jesus is humble of heart and offers us peace.

HUMILITY

The English poet T.S. Eliot once wrote, "Humankind can't stand too much reality." Hence we build illusions which blind us to our true condition. This escape from reality and responsibility is as old as humankind itself. The opening pages of Genesis record the response of Adam and

Eve when confronted by God. Adam blames Eve, and Eve blames the serpent. Both ultimately blame God for having started the whole situation. Clearly an escape from reality and responsibility. As a child, we escape reality by inventing playmates to blame for the neighbor's broken window. Later in life, we blame our parents, school, religion, society, genetic makeup or the zodiac for our misdeeds. This escape from reality and responsibility is motivated by insecurity and feelings of inadequacy. We flee from our true condition. That is, the Bible says we are creatures. Sin results from our unwillingness to be a creature. If only we could be *the* creator, then we would be happy.

The beginning and the end of humility is truth. Truth about ourselves and God belongs to the humble person. Humility has nothing to do with self-debasement or self-hatred. Humility is a true recognition of our origin and destiny. The Bible tells us that we are made for glory since we have been made in God's image and likeness. We are the crown of creation and entrusted with the stewardship of God's handiwork. We are called to reverence all of life which comes from God as a gift. However, we often turn from God and follow our own designs. We see our origin as creature as an insult rather than a call to glory. The Psalmist, by contrast, is filled with awe as he reflects on the dignity of the human person: "What is man that you are mindful of him . . . man that you have crowned him with glory . . . You have made him a little less than the angels" (Psalm 8). Our destiny is to be part of God's Kingdom and share His very life. We do not need to impress God in order to earn His favor. God has given us all we need to live life to the full.

The Israelites began to think that the covenant was a release from justice and obeying God's will. However, the prophet, like Isaiah, reminds the people that the covenant is a call to greater responsibility, justice and love. If much is given, much is expected. Jesus objects to Scribes and Pharisees who use their power not to serve but to be served. They see their leadership as a symbol of pride and boasting. Their words are bold and high sounding, but they fail to act. In fact, Jesus says one should avoid their behavior. The true teacher and great person is one who, in humility and truth, serves the needs of the community. Through such humble service one will be exalted by God. Jesus, the greatest example of love and service, emptied himself of glory and accepted the Cross. In so doing, Jesus completed the work of his Father and was exalted as Lord of lords and King of kings.

Lent is a time when we search for the truth about ourselves and God. We are creatures called to share the very life of God given by Jesus in the Spirit. We are created out of love and called to share God's love. The God who creates, redeems and sustains us is ever faithful. This is the truth that sets us free.

Wednesday of the Second Week
Jeremiah 18:18-20
Matthew 20:17-28

The prophet Jeremiah learns a bitter lesson: even when one does good, one may not receive good in return. In fact, hostility and vengeance often await the prophet. The prophet calls for change and repentance. The people must give up their sinful ways. Jeremiah, like Jesus, is an innocent sufferer at the hands of vengeful people.

Jesus tells the disciples that it is time to go to Jerusalem. It is time for Jesus to suffer and die. Not only must Jesus suffer, but also all who follow him. This was clearly misunderstood by James and John. They wanted to share Jesus' glory, but not his suffering and rejection. They wanted the resurrection, but not the cross. Discipleship is offered, but not the symbols of authority and power. The only true authority of the disciple is that of service.

Such talk of power and prestige begins to disrupt the community. The other disciples want a share in the glory. So be it. But it is not the authority of earthly powers. The disciple must seek to be like the Son of Man—a suffering servant who sacrifices daily for the good of the community.

AMBITION

One of the best things that can be said about Americans is that we are an ambitious people. An essential ingredient in the American character is the willingness to make sacrifices in order to succeed. Part of the American Myth is the belief that by hard work we will make all things better for ourselves and our children. Anyone who is willing and has drive can succeed in this land of unlimited opportunity. To be unambitious is to be un-American. Hence, the request of the mother of Zebedee's sons (James and John) for places of honor may strike us initially as only doing what any good parent would do. However, the Biblical notion of ambition is very different from our modern one.

The Biblical notion of ambition is a willingness to serve the Lord. There is no guarantee of worldly fame, acceptance or rewards. Just the opposite can be expected. To be ambitious in the Lord's service is to court rejection, misunderstanding and the hatred of the world. The prophets are those called to proclaim God's word of repentance and change. They are rejected and even killed because so few people want to give up the old securities and conveniences. Jeremiah finds out firsthand that even though he does good for others, they repay him with evil, and plot to take his life. When Jeremiah prayed for the people so that the Lord's anger would be revoked, they accepted him. However, when Jeremiah called for conversion and repentance, they turned against him.

Jesus teaches the hard lesson of ambition and service in the Kingdom of God. The ambitious member of the Kingdom is one who willingly travels the road to Jerusalem with Jesus. This means a willingness to be rejected by all the respectable people of our day. It is a willingness to seek the glory of God rather than the praise of others. The ambition of the mother of Zebedee's sons represents the values of this world, and the standards of worldly success. She wants them to be given places of honor and reverence. However, to seek honor in the Kingdom means to be a person who can walk with Jesus and drink the cup of the passion. Reverence is accorded to those who give humble service and lovingly meet the needs of others. True and lasting authority in the Christian community always follows the example of Jesus. Jesus is in the midst of his disciple as a servant and the one who goes about doing good. The values of this world are in conflict with the values of the Kingdom.

Lent is the season of preparation for the paschal mystery of the death and resurrection of Jesus. We cannot have one without the other. There can be no rising on the third day unless one is willing to travel to Jerusalem and be crucified. Today we emphasize the positive aspects of Lent and penance. This is certainly in order. However, we can never lose sight of the Cross and its meaning. For the Son of Man came to accept that Cross so that we could be liberated from sin and death. It is for us to accept a share in the Cross so that we too can experience the joy of the resurrection.

Thursday of the Second Week
Jeremiah 17:5-10
Luke 16:19-31

The prophet Jeremiah confronts one of the deepest human concerns: whom can we trust completely? Many trust completely in others. However, there are times when only God can meet our needs. Others turn from God in order to trust in the achievements of culture or in their own efforts. Only the person who trusts in the Lord will never be disappointed. The person whose hope is the Lord is ready to meet every situation in life. It is only the Lord who searches the human heart and knows the good and evil that is present.

The story of the rich man and the beggar Lazarus challenges our assumption about reward and punishment. Many expect the good to prosper and the evil to suffer, in this world and the next. However, the rich man enjoys the good life in this world, but knows only torment in the next. Lazarus, who suffers much, is now resting in the bosom of Abraham. Notice Jesus does not say that Lazarus was a good man and the rich man was evil. Rather, Jesus is challenging our conventional wisdom, judgments and values. The values of the Kingdom reverse the values of this world..This story prevents us from becoming smug and self-assured. God is a God of surprises and does not conform to our standards of justice.

THE UNEXPECTED

Part of the conventional wisdom of Jesus' day was the belief that the good were rewarded by God in this life and the next. If one was rich, healthy and wise it was taken for granted that the person was being blessed by God. Furthermore, once that person died, he would continue being blessed in the next life with God. By contrast, the wicked person suffered in this world. He was judged to be unworthy of association, and deserving of any ill treatment. Naturally, the afterlife was a continuation of his present sufferings. Some religious views even went so far as to say that evil done by past generations could befall the present and future ones. The picture of God presented is not a very attractive one. He seems to be busy dividing the world into good and evil, and giving each what he deserves. There is no room for conversion and comparison. God is just to a fault!

The Old Testament book of Job challenges this perspective. Job is a good and upright man, yet he suffers. At the end of the book, we are left with the great mystery of good and evil. Jesus, in the parable of the rich man and Lazarus, rejects this principle of judgment out of hand. The rich man who feasts splendidly each day is the one who ends in torment. The beggar Lazarus finds himself in the bosom of Abraham. This is a real shocker; a real transvaluation of values. The expected is not realized. The predictable does not occur. Instead, the unexpected happens: the beggar becomes rich in the Lord and the rich man becomes poor. The unexpected is a recurrent theme in the Gospel of St. Luke. In the *Magnificat*, the mighty are expelled from the thrones, and the lowly are given every good thing. Those who mourn and weep will rejoice, and the rich will be sent away empty. Again, Jesus does not explain why Lazarus is in heaven and the rich man is in torment. That is simply the way it is.

In our own society, we often trust in riches and the work

of our hands. We look down on the poor and the lowly. Those who are without work are lazy and deserve to be poor. The evil that befalls others is a just punishment for breaking God's laws. Suffering is something that results from our sins. The conventional wisdom goes on and on. Yet this parable of Jesus calls such 'wisdom' into question. We do not have the insight to search the human heart and know its ways. Only God can do that. In the words of Jeremiah, "the Lord alone probes the mind and tests the heart." The external conditions of this world are often misleading as to the quality of one's relationship with God.

In various ways, Lazarus still lives outside our door. The rich nations of the world continue to consume resources as if they have an absolute right to creation. The poor are still rejected as lazy or deserving of punishment. The rich man did not directly hurt Lazarus; he simply ignored him. Lazarus never entered his everyday world. Lent is a good time to be aware of the Lazarus in our life. A genuine search for God challenges us to find Lazarus as well.

Friday of the Second Week
Genesis 37:3-4, 12-13, 17-28
Matthew 21:33-43, 45-46

The story of Joseph and his beautiful coat speaks to us of the destructive force of envy. Israel loved Joseph the most and gave him a coat to symbolize this love. Joseph's brothers became filled with hatred and envy. These bad feelings so consumed them that they plotted to kill him. Rather than kill Joseph, they decided to sell him into slavery in Egypt for twenty pieces of silver. However, God did not abandon Joseph. During the famine in Egypt, Joseph rose to power through his wisdom. He did not seek vengeance on his brothers, but reconciliation.

This theme of rejection and hatred by loved ones is powerfully expressed in the Gospel. Jesus is the Son of God sent to bring good news to the people. Instead of being accepted, Jesus is rejected, plotted against and killed. One of his own disciples betrays him for thirty pieces of silver. The Father does not abandon Jesus, but raises him from the dead on the third day. How tragic the rejection of Jesus! He came to give the Kingdom of God to Israel, but only found hostility. Now the rejected stone has become the cornerstone for the Gentiles and all who confess that Jesus is Lord.

THE BEAUTIFUL COAT

As we read the story of Joseph and his envious brothers, we naturally condemn the brothers' reactions. They have no right to act that way toward Joseph. His father Israel loves him the best, and gives a beautiful coat to express this love.

Why can't the brothers accept this? Or better, why can't they strive to be more like Joseph? Maybe Israel would make them a coat as well. However, if we pause long enough to come off of our moralizing pedestal, we find ourselves feeling and acting much like Joseph's brothers. We all have memories of those times when our performance was measured against a relative or friend. We were filled with *pride* if our work was superior. We were filled with *bitterness* if such a comparison left us on the short end. Either way, we lost in every comparison. We come to see our worth in terms of achievements, and judge others on the basis of their works. There is not much room for grace, gifts and sharing. Everyone's loss is my gain, and my loss is another's gain. Life is filled with the struggle to compete and grasp all the beautiful coats.

Without getting into why Israel loved Joseph best, he simply did and he did give the coat. The brothers gave in to envy. We commonly call envy the 'green-eyed monster' since it blinds and consumes those held under its power. Envy is one of the capital or deadly sins, since it kills our ability to see the giftedness of all life. Envy consumes our hearts with hatred and drives out all feelings of love and compassion. Hence, envy makes violence and killing all too easy. Cain kills Abel because Abel finds favor with God. The brothers of Joseph sell him into slavery because of the loving gift of Israel. Jesus is rejected by his own people and handed over to the Romans in order to be killed.

Jesus was sent by the Father to proclaim the good news of salvation. The blind were to see; the lame would walk; and the poor would have the good news preached to them. Those imprisoned by the brokenness of life would be liberated and healed. So why the hostility? Because some took the good news and made it bad news. The good news of Jesus is the call to change and begin to live in the presence of God's Kingdom. This upsets the self-righteous, the smug and the too comfortable. The good news of Jesus challenges the worldly principalities and powers, and calls them to conversion. Above all, the good news of Jesus calls *all* people to be part of God's Kingdom. No one need live alone, separate or alienated. Jesus has overcome sin and the divisions sin causes. We can all live like brothers and sisters in God's family. However, those who want to hold on to the old divisions of good and evil respond with violence. How can salvation be given to the tax collectors, poor fishermen, prostitutes and sinners? Envy and fear of a loss of privilege blind the self-righteous to the fact that no one is included in God's Kingdom at the expense of another.

Envy can disturb our peace and blind us to the many gifts God has given us. Envy eats away at our heart and prevents us from loving others. Envy prevents us from working with others to build a better world. However, in God's Kingdom all are offered beautiful coats.

Saturday of the Second Week
Micah 7:14-15, 18-20
Luke 15:1-3, 11-32

An essential aspect of Israel's history is the theme of wandering and searching for God. In order to guide their journey, Yahweh has always raised up good leaders (Moses, Joshua, David, etc.). The journey is successful as long as the leaders and the people remain faithful to the covenant. However, when the people sin and go astray, destruction follows. The prophet Micah prays for the Lord to guide Israel as He did during the Exodus. Above all, God the Good Shepherd is a God who pardons sins and forgives the people of sin. In effect, Yahweh always remains faithful to the covenant and is always ready to show compassion to Israel.

The theme of journeying and finding a home is beautifully presented by St. Luke in the parable of the Forgiving Father (Prodigal Son). The young son must experience life firsthand, so he leaves home in search of happiness. After some shattering experiences, he comes to his senses (grace) and returns home. The Father is filled with joy and jubilation. The lost son has been found; the one who was dead now lives. Unfortunately, the older son cannot celebrate and rejoice. There is no room in his heart for forgiveness. However, God our forgiving Father always celebrates when we turn from sin and journey to our true home—the Kingdom of God.

A DISTANT LAND

One of the best parts of summer vacation is the ability to travel. There is something about traveling that appeals to our adventurous self. Far away places, strange sounding names, and the lure of the different attracts us. We can leave the familiar and head into the unknown. For the more intellectual, traveling affords the opportunity to study different cultures and histories firsthand. Travel opens our minds and broadens our understanding of the ways of others. Then, of course, there is the traveling that is simply escapist. We want to get away from it all. By traveling we can distance ourselves from the office routine and the telephone. For a week or two we are unreachable. There are as many reasons for traveling as there are places to see. But in the end, we are glad to return home.

Jesus tells a story about a young man who travels to a distant land. Unfortunately, in the words of Sartre he is a 'traveler without a ticket.' He does not have the experience to be a world traveler. He claims more than he has a right to. He wants the inheritance before his father is dead. He travels to a distant land and gets an education in the school of hard knocks. All his dreams are broken, and so he must complete the round trip home. No doubt he expected a cold, 'I told you so' father. Much to his surprise, his father rushes to greet him and calls for a grand celebration. The rehearsed apology of the son is ignored. The relationship that was broken is now reestablished. To the father, his young son as always is his son, and nothing more need be said. All of the expected self-demeaning statements are out of place. All that is important is that life has been triumphant over death, and the distant land has led homeward. To travel you need a ticket. To come home all you need is the map of repentance.

Unfortunately, the son who stayed home has no room for mercy. He has slaved for his father all these years, and has never received even a goat. While he has slaved for him, he obviously has not loved his father. His sense of duty has become merely a formalistic obedience without a loving spirit. In many ways, this second son is the prodigal. He really doesn't have a home—he only *slaves* for the father. He knows nothing of family life—the need for joy, celebration and forgiveness. Jesus tells this parable in response to the respectable folk who are shocked by his table fellowship with sinners and tax collectors. How can Jesus associate with such folk? Simple: it is for the sinner and the outcast that Jesus has come; not to announce judgment, but forgiveness and celebration. This is God's way.

The American novelist Thomas Wolfe warns that we can't go home again. Much to our benefit, we can always return to God and our true home. We need not worry about the reception. Jesus tells us clearly that it will be one of joy and great rejoicing. You can go home again. All we need to do is come to our senses and return to the love of our Father. The music and dancing have already started.

Third Week of Lent

Monday of the Third Week
2 Kings 5:1-15
Luke 4:24-30

"Now I know that there is no God in all the earth, except in Israel." Are these the words of Moses, David, Solomon, or some pious Jew? No. These are the words of gratitude and acknowledgement proclaimed by Naaman after being healed of leprosy. Naaman is a Gentile. The cure of Naaman is a foresign of the healing work of Jesus. God is not the exclusive claim of any nation. Rather, Yahweh is the Lord of all people and heals those who turn to him in obedience and faith.

Jesus returns home to Nazareth and teaches in the synagogue. However, he is met with rejection. The words of the prophet are not welcomed in his home town. Jesus uses Israel's history to remind the people of what happens when one rejects a prophet. During the great famine in Israel, Elijah was sent to the widow of Zarephath. Of the many lepers in Israel, only one was cured, namely, Naaman the Syrian. Both the widow of Zarephath and Naaman were 'outsiders' and considered 'unholy.' The people of the promise have closed their hearts to God's word and the covenant. Now the promises will be given to those who were far off, but are now drawn into salvation.

THE CHOSEN ONES

Most of us have had the experience of choosing sides in a baseball game—the tossing of the bat back and forth to see which captain gets first choice. To be chosen first is a real childhood badge of honor. No one wants to be the last pick (the 'sure out' kid). If we were not into athletics, we may have had the opportunity to make out the guest list for a big party. Part of the fun is in choosing who will and will NOT be invited. Each of us knows well the joy of being invited and the hurt of being passed over. In adult life, the process of choosing and being overlooked is still operative. The stakes are just higher. It no longer involves baseball games and parties but jobs and career advancement. The Scriptures talk a great deal about vocation and being chosen. Instead of God choosing the strong, fast, agile, intelligent, wealthy, powerful and beautiful people, He chooses the lowly and the weak. God calls those who have no resources or apparent talents. He makes a covenant with the wretched of the earth.

Yahweh chooses an insignificant group of wanderers and calls them to be His people. They will be the chosen ones through whom God's justice will be revealed. God chooses the lowly and makes them strong in order to prevent their boasting. The lowly and the weak know that it is only through God's power that they are what they are. The rich and powerful rely too much on their own resources. The rich become smug and arrogant. Unfortunately, the Israelites come to see their election as a call to privilege rather than responsibility and obedience. They come to see everyone who is not part of the Jewish nation as unworthy of respect and salvation. Salvation is only for the Jews, and everyone else is unholy. Yahweh is their God and no one else's. The Gentiles will die in their sins. The notions of covenant and election give rise to nationalism and religious prejudice.

The story of Naaman serves to challenge this too narrow view of election. Naaman is cured because he is obedient to the words of Elisha the prophet. God does not limit his care and love only to the Jews. Israel was chosen to be God's means of bringing salvation to the whole world. God's Kingdom is not one of exclusion but inclusion. God cannot be owned by any one nation or people. All that is, belongs to the Lord, and is meant to give Him praise. Jesus comes in to his own to announce the good news of salvation. However, he is met with hostility and violence. Therefore, Jesus now extends his ministry of the Kingdom to the Gentiles. The death and resurrection of Jesus is the ultimate expression of God's loving will for all people. The Church will now continue the universal mission of the new covenant.

The gift of knowing Jesus is not a cause for boasting or arrogance. It is a call to deeper love and service. As members of Christ's Body, we are called to transcend the divisions of race, nation and religion. We are to see that what unites us is God's love for all His people. Through our Baptism we have been chosen to reveal to all people the love of God. We work and hope for that day when Christ will be all in all.

Tuesday of the Third Week
Daniel 3:25, 34-43
Matthew 18:21-35

During the time of Daniel the most powerful nation was Babylon, and the most powerful king was Nebuchadnezzar. The king had a statue made and ordered the people to worship it. However, Shadrach, Meshach and Abednego (Azariah) refused. They were thrown into the fire. With great confidence, Azariah prayed to the Lord for strength and deliverance. God is faithful, and in times of distress will not forget His promises. Azariah was willing to suffer and die rather than worship false gods. But deep in his heart, Azariah knew that the Lord would not let him be put to shame.

This good and faithful God sends His Son, Jesus, with good news of salvation. The long reign of sin and death has been broken. God has forgiven us and called us into His love. God not only forgives us but expects us to forgive one another. There is no limit to God's forgiveness. Jesus calls us to practice the same forgiveness. We must be willing to forgive one another from our hearts. We cannot be friends with God if we fail to be reconciled with one another.

MARTYRDOM

Ours is an age that courts the loud and spectacular. Cluttering the contemporary landscape are superstars and superdomes, all built and hyped on the premise that the biggest is the best. At first blush, our reading from Daniel seems to appeal to the modern lust for the flashy. Three young men are told to worship the golden statue or else (the

'else' being the oven waiting to consume those who dis-
obey). The plot thickens as the three are fed into the oven.
However, our hero Azariah stands up in the fires and prays
for divine deliverance. Naturally, the Lord responds. The
three young men are set free and live happily ever after.

The Biblical meaning of this story is much deeper than a
Hollywood spectacular. It is simple and profound: God acts
on behalf of His people. The God of the Bible is the God
who intervenes to care for and protect those who turn to
Him in need. The God of Azariah is One who is faithful to
His promises, and comes with power to sustain those who
face the fires of destruction. Azariah and his two friends
refused to be pressured into idol worship. They stood up to
the earthly principalities and powers rather than turn away
from the God of Abraham and the Exodus. The fidelity of
these three young men is matched in abundance by the
kindness and mercy of the Lord who responds and saves.

In our own daily struggle to follow the Lord and grow
deeper into relationship with Jesus, we face the fires of
everyday life. Our struggles are often unspectacular and not
well known. We often witness to the Gospel in great hiddenness away from the eye of the camera. Ours is the faith
that is known to God alone. Yet the tensions and the need to
be resolute are no less real. The young person who rejects
the peer pressure to drug and alcohol abuse and irresponsible sexuality, suffers a great deal. He or she is often banished
from the crowd and labeled in various uncomplimentary
ways. The businessman who is honest in word and deed and
the worker who gives an honest day's labor, strike a blow for
justice. The mother who each day tries to make a house a
home exhibits great faith, which too often goes un-
recognized. In our Gospel, Jesus calls us to forgive one

another with the depth and breadth that God has forgiven us. Anyone who tries to forgive from the heart not once, but over and over, knows well the suffering required. In all of these instances and many more, there is a suffering and a martyrdom taking place. Such lives of faith and struggle seldom, if ever, make the evening news or the talk shows. That's not important. What is crucial is that such lives are remembered by God and written in the book of life.

At times we can acutely feel the burdens of living the Gospel. These burdens become more trying when we experience so little support and recognition. In fact, we are often ignored or rejected as a dreamer or even as being dangerous. Yet the Psalmist and Jesus speak to our world-weary hearts. "In your kindness remember me, because of your goodness, O Lord" (Ps 25:7). "I am with you always even until the end of the world" (Mt 28:20).

Wednesday of the Third Week
Deuteronomy 4:1, 5-9
Matthew 5:17-19

*Moses calls the Israelites to assembly, and prepares
them to receive the two great gifts of Yahweh. The Lord
gives His people the Law and the land. They need both.
To enter the land without God's law would be to invite
chaos. To give the law without the means to obey it
would be fruitless. God's great love for Israel is present
in these two gifts. Moses reminds the people of their
responsibility for the law and the land. They must obey
the laws and teach them to their children. Only then
will they grow into a great and wise nation.*

*Jesus does not come as a rebel or a preacher of
shock-theology. Rather, Jesus comes to complete and
perfect the law and the prophets. God's law and the
prophetic word can be dismissed as unimportant. The
law and the prophets are given to Israel to guide and
keep the people in the Lord's ways. Jesus comes as the
New Moses proclaiming the New Law of love and
grace, Jesus is the ultimate prophet who comes to
announce the good news of salvation. Now is the time
to repent and reform, for the Kingdom is at hand!*

LAW AND PROPHETS

It is hard to think of two more misunderstood and unappreciated aspects of the Old Testament than the law and the
prophets. We modern children of the Enlightenment, who
have come of age on the milk of democracy, liberalism and
the will to power have a rather negative view of the law. Law
is viewed as that which restricts our freedom and inhibits the

doing of our own thing. The law, and its accessory in slavery, tradition, keep us from acting like adults and standing on our own. The law is nothing but a series of don'ts, which is given by the elite (political and religious) to keep the rest of us in bondage.

The stereotypical view of the prophet is no better. The prophet is a rather strange person who is anti-social, anti-human, and definitely anti-fun. The prophet lives in constant fear that somewhere someone is having a good time! His words are filled with judgment and anger. Naturally, this is a rather unfair and one-sided reading of the law and the prophets. If we can lower our modern assumptions, perhaps we can understand these two gifts of Israel.

Gifts! The law and prophets can't be gifts. Can they? From the perspective of the Bible, they are precious gifts and proof that God loves His people. The law and the prophets are essential to the religious vision of Israel. The Lord has delivered His people, cared for them in the desert, and led them into the promised land. Yahweh doesn't stop here. Through Moses, Yahweh reveals His will and plan for the well-being of Israel. Yahweh has not revealed Himself to another people. What is most shocking is that Yahweh, unlike any other god, enters into covenant with His people. Yahweh is not a hidden god who stays in heaven and ignores the events of history. He is the Lord of history, and acts mightily on behalf of Israel. God acts. God cares. God loves. God is not indifferent or aloof, but again and again seeks the people out when they go astray. The prophets are not messengers of angry words (though their words are angry), but words of passion. The prophets passionately want to remind the people how much God loves them, and will be satisfied with nothing less than their total response. The God who acts, cares and loves is demanding.

Jesus comes to complete and perfect the gifts of the law and the prophetic word. The law revealed through Moses was a foretaste of the new covenant. The new covenant, revealed by Jesus in his death and resurrection, liberates us from sin and death. The new covenant is the revelation of just how much God acts, cares and loves us. The God who speaks from the burning bush now takes on a human face in Jesus. The eternal has become temporal, and God has become human. The prophetic word of Jesus is, "repent, reform, believe, for the good news of the Kingdom is here in your midst." In the words of Father Andrew Greeley, "On Sinai we learned that God loves us; in the cross and resurrection we learned how much he loves us."

The God who first gave us the law and the prophets, and brings them to perfection in Jesus, is no ordinary God. In fact, there is none like him in all the universe. Our God is one who acts, cares and loves. Moreover, He expects us to love Him with our whole being and care for one another. Nothing less is required or acceptable.

Thursday of the Third Week
Jeremiah 7:23-28
Luke 11:14-23

The role of the Hebrew prophet is to continually call the people back to their covenant relationship with Yahweh. This call to covenant fidelity is always expressed in light of the Exodus experience. It was Yahweh who delivered them out of slavery, provided for their wilderness needs, and brought them safely into the promised land. However, the people forget the Exodus and the covenant. They turn to idol worship and grow hard of heart. The task of the prophet is never easy. Even though Jeremiah proclaims the Lord's word, the people will not listen. Faithfulness is gone from the land.

Jesus cast out a devil and frees the man to speak. However, instead of praising God, some of the people accuse Jesus of being in partnership with the devil. Others demand signs as if the casting out of devils is insignificant. Jesus rejects this and says that it is by the power of God that Satan is driven out. The people are blinded to the workings of God through Jesus. We cannot cast our allegiance with the world and with Jesus. We must decide. "The man who is not with me is against me. The man who does not gather with me scatters."

HARDNESS OF HEART

Throughout our Lenten journey, with its call to conversion and rebirth, we have heard much of what blocks our search for God. Sin and the illusions of happiness blind us to the God who also is in search of us. Sin and idolatry are real, but the Really Real is the covenant of compassion and mercy offered by the God of love. The God who revealed Himself at Sinai and Bethlehem is the God who walks with us in the valley of darkness, and who fills in the rough spots of our heart. Simply put: Yahweh-Jesus is a faithful God who wants to share His life with us.

However great and powerful God's love and mercy, the human heart cannot be ignored. The love, compassion and mercy of God can only find a place in the heart that is receptive and willing to respond. Humankind's refusal to listen to God's word is nothing new. Adam and Eve, Pharaoh, the murmuring Israelites in the desert, the Israelites of Jeremiah's time, and the crowd that confronts Jesus all refuse to respond to God's gracious presence. The New Testament speaks of the 'sin against the Holy Spirit,' and the First Letter of John talks about the 'sin unto death.' The Scriptures are aware that the human heart can indeed be a block of stone, deaf to the transforming word of the Lord. Yahweh's love is never more evident than in His respect for human freedom. Hardness of heart is our refusal to let God in, but the Scriptures also tell us that Yahweh-Jesus never gives up without a fight. Our God is indeed like Francis Thompson's *Hound of Heaven.*

Jeremiah speaks God's word of renewal and the need to come home to the covenant. Unfortunately, the Israelites come to believe that all they need do is worship God in an external, formalistic way without an inward change of heart. However, such is not the case. To offer sacrifice without a change of heart finds no acceptance with the Lord. The people in the hardness of their hearts are really engaging in self-worship. Jesus in our Gospel comes to heal the sick, preach the good news, and free those in the grip of the devil. All of this is the sign that God's Kingdom is now at work. However, the people refuse to see and believe. They remain blind to the working of God through Jesus. The good works that he does are interpreted as the acts of Satan. They hear his voice, see his works, but harden their hearts.

A hard heart is not confined to the pages of Scripture. Hardness of heart can all too easily blind us to the workings of God in our own life. We can refuse to give up self-worship. We fail to see how each day is a gift and a miracle of God's unbounded love. We too often ask what God is going to do for us, rather than ask what are we to do in order to give thanks to the Lord for all he has done for us. Hardness of heart can blind us to the gifts and talents of others. We fail to see their possibilities and abilities for the common good. Hardness of heart can keep us from reconciliation with God and those whom we love. We just can't make the first move. To do so would be a sign of weakness and the admission that we were wrong. Hardness of heart need not be terminal. The Holy Spirit blows where it wills. With the Psalmist we cry, "Create in us, O Lord, a heart renewed. Recreate in us your own Spirit." Amen.

Friday of the Third Week
Hosea 14:2-10
Mark 12:28-34

The book of the prophet Hosea uses the imagery of marriage to speak of God's relationship with His people. Israel is often like an unfaithful wife. She continues to forget the mighty deeds of Yahweh, and chases after idols. However, Yahweh is forever faithful. God is not passive or aloof, but actively seeks Israel and wants to ''speak tenderly to her heart.'' The real security and hope of Israel is not to be found in military alliances (Assyria) or human achievement. Rather, the compassionate and mighty God who was present at the Red Sea and Sinai is her hope. The words of Hosea end on a note of confidence. Yahweh will heal their defection and turn from His wrath, so that they can grow and be fruitful.

The theme of God's love reaches completion in Jesus. Those who are members of God's Kingdom must be a people of love. First, we must love God with our whole being. Second, we must love our neighbor as we love ourselves. This is the acceptable sacrifice to God. Jesus' words remind us that authentic love has three movements: God, neighbor and self. We know what authentic love is through the words and deeds of Jesus. Love is the willingness to lay down one's life for the neighbor. Love is the total worship of God. Love is the proper regard for the gift of our life. Love calls us to offer the true and lasting sacrifice—the gift of the self. Through love we extend God's reign.

LOVE: THE REAL THING

Ralph Waldo Emerson once said about some dinner guests, "The more and more they proclaimed their honesty and virtue, the more and more I counted the silverware." Emerson has touched upon an all too common aspect of life: the more we talk about something, the less substance and results seem to follow. We often drift into extremes in discussing complex dimensions of human behavior. For example, we either avoid all talk about human sexuality or we trivialize it by making it the 'hidden persuader' in selling automobiles and toothpaste. We are uncomfortable talking about death, so we deny its reality in our love affair with the Pepsi Generation of eternal youth. It seems the more and more we talk about something, the less we understand. This is certainly true of love. There seems to be so little real love behind all the talk of love. What more is there to say to a society that believes the last word on love is contained in the following: "Love means you never have to say you're sorry"? Hopefully, we have a great deal to say. The witness of Hosea and Jesus does.

Today, we often equate love with feelings and emotions. Love is equated with the feelings of physical attraction toward the other. Our images of love are provided by the soap opera and the prime time skin flick that passes for adult entertainment. The lesson to be learned about love as feeling, emotion, physical attraction and sexual performance is that love is seldom if ever permanent. Feelings and emotions change rapidly. Physical attraction and sexual performance soon become boring. What we are left with are quick exchanges of the most superficial kind. The

Scriptures, by contrast, speak of authentic love as creative, liberating and sustaining.

One of the oldest of human questions is, 'Why is there something rather than nothing?' From the perspective of the Bible the answer is, 'Because God is love and love is creative.' God creates and recreates out of love. Love is extensional and reaches out. Love brings forth the new, the creative, and rejoices with the possible. God's very nature as love required creation. Love also liberates and frees the other to realize possibilities. The decisive moment in Israel's history is the Exodus experience. God's love is a love which frees one to be the best one can be. We are fully alive to the extent that we live in love and freedom. The ultimate symbols of love and liberation are the cross and the empty tomb. Love is never for the moment, but is faithful, enduring, permanent and sustaining. Yahweh never forgets His people, and continually calls them back to the covenant. In the words of Hosea, ''Return, O Israel, to the Lord, your God.'' Jesus does not leave the disciples orphans. He sends the Paraclete to guide, teach, strengthen and encourage the community.

The wisdom of the world understands love to be silent about the need for forgiveness. However, the wisdom of the world is foolishness to God. Christian love recognizes the need to forgive and accept forgiveness. In confidence, we can turn to the God who is Love, and seek healing from our sins. We need never fear, for love drives out all fear and anxiety from our hearts. Perhaps it was said best by St. Paul, ''There is no limit to love's ability to forgive, to trust, to hope, and to endure.''

Saturday of the Third Week
Hosea 6:1-6
Luke 18:9-14

The prophet Hosea continues his message of love and healing. The Israelites know that their afflictions are the result of turning from the Lord. Yahweh loves them completely, but they must accept the consequences of their actions. The seeking of reconciliation with the Lord can never be merely external or formalistic. It must be a complete change of heart. The sacrifices of animals will not find acceptance. What Yahweh requires is love and an inward turning of the heart. Only then will the people experience a binding of their wounds, a healing of hearts, and the revival of broken spirits.

The Pharisees were self-righteous and smug in holding to their superiority over others. They knew how to pray, fast and give money. However, they do not possess what is most required: humility and the need to acknowledge their sinfulness. By contrast, the tax collector has only one thing to give, a humble and contrite heart. He is aware of his sins, but is more aware of God's forgiving love. Jesus says that the tax collector finds favor with God, while the Pharisee does not. Once again, St. Luke turns our expectations upside down. The self-exalted are brought low, and the poor in spirit are healed and given every good thing.

THE CENTER OF THINGS

Most of us at one time or another have come under the influence of a teacher or professor. While studying philosophy at Tulane University, I came under the positive influence of Professor Edward G. Ballard. Professor Ballard directed my thesis on Martin Heidegger and Rudolf Bultmann. One day, I asked Professor Ballard what he had learned from his study of philosophy. What was the one bit of golden wisdom that life and study had revealed most clearly to him? I expected some deep philosophical response extending over many minutes. Naturally that's not what I got. Professor Ballard said simply, "Long ago I decided not to be the center of things." This simple piece of wisdom has never left me. In many ways, our readings today and the Christian life say the same thing: don't be at the center of things. Well, if I am not to be the center of things, then who is?

The history of Israel's religious journey is one of answering this question. Yahweh is the Lord of the covenant, and the One who forms them as a people. However, Israel is not always faithful. Yahweh is displaced now and then, much to Israel's regret and Yahweh's sorrow. The prophets, such as Hosea, continually remind the people that Yahweh must be the center and heart of their life. Israel's piety must be more lasting than the morning cloud and the dew that early passes away. What the Lord requires is that His love be at the center of things.

Jesus contrasts the prayer life of two men with two very different centers of meaning. The Pharisee is self-righteous. He is at the center of things. The predominant word in his prayers is 'I.' The imperial ego is at the center, and there is no room for God or others. In fact, he is most grateful that he is not like the rest of humankind—sinful. The tax collector is the man of true prayer. His prayer comes from the recognition that he is a sinner and in need of forgiveness. He does not multiply his words, simply trusts that God will hear him and respond. Jesus indicates that the tax collector goes home justified. The Pharisee is a wanderer, and can never find the peace that comes with having God as the center of life.

The happiness and integrity of our lives often swing on the answer we give as to who is the center of things. An intimate friendship or loving marriage require that the ego move over and make room for the other. If we never make room for others, our relationships are shallow and short-lived. Marriage demands that we shift our vocabulary from 'I' to 'we'; from 'mine' to 'ours'; from 'you' to 'us.' The Christian life and subsequent happiness result from shared existence and the realization of how much we are like the rest of humankind.

To not be at the center of things may cause us anxiety and insecurity. If I am not for me, who will be? If I don't look out for number one, who will? I have to be my own best friend, don't I? All these questions melt away once we realize that God is for us and with us. Jesus is the ultimate proof that we are not forgotten. In letting God be at the center of our lives, we are greatly exalted.

Fourth Week of Lent

Monday of the Fourth Week
Isaiah 65:17-21
John 4:43-54

In our religious devotion, it is always important to keep a sense of balance. Lent can be viewed as a time of gloom and doom. However, Isaiah speaks to us of great hope and joy. Yahweh is not a God of the past, but the Lord of all history—past, present and future. Above all, Yahweh is the God who does new things. He not only creates, but recreates and renews. Isaiah challenges us not to be victims of our past sins and failures. God's grace liberates us for the future. We are to live in joy and peace and hope, keeping our hearts set on the new Jerusalem. We wait in patient hope for the time in which God creates the new heavens and a new earth.

The intervention of the new in history is totally present in Jesus. Jesus is the Word made flesh, sent by the Father to make His name known. Jesus performs seven signs in the Fourth Gospel. The healing of the royal official's son in our present reading is the second of these signs. Notice that his own people do not believe in Jesus unless they see signs. By contrast, the official believes on the words of Jesus. He exhibits authentic faith. A constant theme throughout the Fourth Gospel is the rejection of Jesus by the Jewish leaders, and the surprising acceptance of Jesus by outsiders. Jesus comes unto his own but they refuse to receive him. How tragic.

THE NEW CREATION

As we read the newspaper and watch the evening news, we realize that something is wrong. Humankind was never meant to live that way. Wars, pollution, violence, death, injustice and hatred were not part of God's initial plan. Yes, something went wrong, and many believe things will only get worse. Today we witness the rise of people called 'survivalists.' They store up food and supplies in a desert hideout protected by guns, ready to meet the impending doom. Most of us, in less dramatic ways, simply dream of simpler, more peaceful times when God was in his heaven and all was well with the world. Perhaps this is why nostalgia exerts such a strong influence on us. The future is dark and getting darker. There must have been a time of paradise when everything was perfect.

This hankering after the good old days of morality and faith is a luxury we Christians can't afford. Through baptism and the laboring of the Holy Spirit in the whole creation, we are called to actively, responsibly work to renew the face of the earth. The Christian is a person of hope, one who is at home in the complexities of history. We cherish our past. We work in the present. We hope for the future. Our vocation is to work with God's Spirit who brings about a new heaven and a new earth. God liberates us from the slavery of our past sins and guilt. We are to be a people of joy and happiness. We work and wait in hope for that time when there will be no more weeping, no death of the newborn, no wasted lives when the elderly will not be rejected, and everyone will find a home to be filled with good things. This is quite a vision presented by Isaiah, a great insight into the God we worship.

The work of the new creation is fully present in Jesus. He comes to proclaim that the long reign of sin and death has been broken. We are now to live as new creatures in the new creation. This is not a human achievement of victory, but God's work of love and renewal. Our task is to be co-workers and continue the work of Jesus through the Spirit. By our everyday Christian witness to faith and justice, we continue the work of the new creation. Each time we speak on behalf of justice, a small part of the world is transformed. Each time we lift our voices and talents on behalf of life, we proclaim the name of the One who comes to give life to the full. Each time we spend our energies helping others find a home and the good things of life, we do the work of our loving Father.

Lent is the season of the new creation. We may be held in the slavery of the past. Our sins and our rejection of God and neighbors may weigh heavy on our hearts. We need not despair. We need not let our past determine our present or future. The God who creates is also the God who recreates and liberates. The sacrament of reconciliation is God's abiding presence as forgiving love. This sacrament continues to speak to us new life and healing. Another prophet, Ezekiel, speaks of the new creation, "I will give you a new heart and place a new spirit within you, taking from your bodies your stony hearts and giving you hearts of flesh" (Ezk 36:26).

Tuesday of the Fourth Week
Ezekiel 47:1-9, 12
John 5:1-3, 5-16

Ezekiel appeals to two great symbols of Israel's religious tradition: the Temple and water. The Temple was the central place of Jewish worship, where one could give thanks and praise to the living God. Through Temple worship, one could offer sacrifices and ask for the things one needed. The Temple came to symbolize God's faithful presence with His people. From the Temple flows life-giving water. Water brings life to the land and subsequently to the people. It is important to remember that this life-giving water is a free gift from God's love. It is not something that we earn, but rather is God's free gift of grace.

In our reading from John, we witness a story of God's intervention in response to human persistence. A man who had been sick for thirty-eight years went to the Sheep Pool each day to be healed. However, someone always arrived ahead of him. This day, when all hope had been lost and the same results were expected, Jesus does something new. Not only does he cure the man, but he tells him to turn to God and give up sinning. When human resources reach their limit, God acts with power. The response of the authorities is predictable. They begin to persecute him.

GRACIOUSNESS

Each age has its own view of the world, and raises up ''the reality policemen'' who say what is true, beautiful and good. In the last two hundred years, we have come to form a worldview which is in conflict with the Biblical perspective. Today's worldview places a high premium on control, power, security and economic clout. Each day is a challenge to prove one's usefulness by consuming and producing goods and services. Our relationships are valued in terms of effectiveness and career pay-offs. We value the other only inasmuch as he or she can help us be successful in our profession. We value upward mobility and getting ahead, often at the expense of others. The rule of the day is competition not cooperation. My personal worth is in what I have, produce and spend. Those who are unable to consume or produce are not deserving of respect. In fact, what little they have should be taken from them! Psychiatrist Erich Fromm once asked, "If I am what I have, but all that I have is taken from me, what then am I?" Simple: Nothing.

Our readings from Ezekiel and the Fourth Gospel challenge this modern perspective. Both of our readings place a maximum premium on graciousness and the giftedness of existence. Both reject the idea that it is of utmost importance to be in control, have power and predict every outcome. Above all, our readings reject the idea that life is based on merit. Rather, they affirm the graciousness and giftedness of life. In the words of Father Chardin, "there is something alive in the universe; something like gestation and birth." Ezekiel tells us that water flowed from the Temple. Water is a symbol of life and abundance. No one can control or predict the waters of life. They are not earned, but received in gratitude. Yahweh is a gracious and loving God.

The graciousness of God is clearly shown in the healing of the cripple at the Sheep Pool. For thirty-eight years the cripple has been sick, and no one responded to his needs. No doubt today would be like all other days—futile, filled with pain, and overlooked by others seeking their own needs. Much to the surprise of all present, today would be different. The lame would walk, and the good news of salvation would be preached to this outcast. Just when all seems lost, or we are at the limit of our resources, God acts on our behalf. God intervenes to save and heal His people. No one spoke or moved to help him, so God had to act.

Not only is the God of Ezekiel and the Father of Jesus a gracious and caring God, but He requires of His people the same compassion and kindness. As we have been given, so we are to give. Since we have been forgiven, we are to forgive the debts of others. The Christian is not one who relates to others on the basis of merits, but on the basis of need. The God who responds to the needs of Israel in the desert, and Jesus who moves to cure the sick, expect the same from us. Each day we have the opportunity to respond to the needs of those who are overlooked in a world of achievers. We can 'walk wet' in our baptismal waters by bringing life to those who despair, and restore the heart of those brought low. Ours is a gracious God, and we are to be His gracious people.

Wednesday of the Fourth Week
Isaiah 49:8-15
John 5:17-30

The most destructive effect of sin is the alienation of humankind from God, creation and one another. Sin divides and breaks the bond of unity that was part of God's initial plan for creation. However, sin does not have the last word. Isaiah presents a magnificent vision of healing and restoration. Israel has been brought low by forgetting the covenant. But now comes deliverance. The day of salvation and restoration is at hand. The imprisoned are liberated. The barren produce fruit. The arid land is filled with water. The rough edges of life are made smooth. All of this is done because Yahweh is faithful to His promises. Yahweh is like a faithful mother who shows tenderness to her children. Yahweh never forgets those in need.

The God who is faithful to His covenant brings it to completion in the sending of the Word. Jesus, the Word made flesh, comes to reveal the Father and do His will. The work of the Father and Jesus is the same: to bring the divine life of love to all who believe. The disciples are called to continue this work of making God present by faith in Jesus and love for one another. To believe in Jesus as the Son of God is to experience eternal life— now! Jesus is the new and eternal covenant of life. This covenant is offered to all who believe that Jesus is the Son of God.

ETERNAL LIFE

One of the most enduring dreams of the human spirit is the quest for the fountain of youth and the secret to eternal life. If only Adam and Eve had not eaten the fruit, who knows, we might never have to taste death. Wouldn't it be wonderful to live forever? Wouldn't it be grand not to have to grow old and die? At first blush, the answer seems to be yes. There is a little of Ponce de Leon in all of us. Yet in our more reflective moments, to live forever may not be all it seems to be. To grow old does not mean that we necessarily grow wise. We may just grow older. The pains and sufferings of life would still be around. There would simply be no end to our days. It is never enough to add days to our life without experiencing life to our days. The mythic search for eternal life is very different from the Biblical version.

Jesus tells the Jews, "The man who hears my word and has faith in him who sent me possesses eternal life." From the perspective of the Fourth Gospel, eternal life is our personal faith commitment that Jesus is the Son of God and the one who reveals the Father as suffering love. Authentic faith is contrasted with inauthentic faith. Inauthentic faith is belief in Jesus because of the signs he performs. Such a 'faith' understands Jesus as a miracle worker. As long as he is doing some mighty deed, all is well. However, when the miracles stop or don't fit the pattern we expect, faith is withheld. The one who believes only in signs is not really a person of faith.

By contrast, authentic faith is our personal encounter and belief in the person of Jesus as the Christ. We do not base our belief on signs, but on the words of Jesus who is "the way, the truth and the life." The signs that Jesus works are indicators of God's active presence in the world. Through the miracles of healing, forgiving sins and even raising the dead, Jesus is showing us that God continues to be with and for His people. We do not believe in the sign, but in the loving, powerful, active God who is present. To believe in the signs is idolatry. True faith is expressed in our relationship with Jesus as the One sent by the Father as the Savior of the whole world.

For the person who believes in Jesus already has eternal life as a gift of the Son. Eternal life is not a gift we receive at the end of the world or when we die. The true believer has already passed from death to life, and does not come under condemnation. The disciple of Jesus is one who lives each day in freedom, love and joy. The disciple is free from the bondage of sin and all that keeps one from living life to the full. The disciple is a person of love in imitation of Jesus— love incarnate. The disciple is a person of joy, since the Paraclete dwells in our hearts. We are filled with the gifts that gladden our spirit.

Eternal life is not the endless possession of marks on a calendar. Eternal life is a whole new way of living and being in the world. We live no longer for ourselves, but to love God and serve our neighbor. Eternal life is a gift already given, and a promise of what our loving God has in store for us. Jesus is offering us, now and in the future, life to the full. With Jesus there is something greater than even Ponce de Leon!

Thursday of the Fourth Week
Exodus 32:7-14
John 5:1-47

Moses has guided the Israelites out of bondage in Egypt. He has kept the Lord's word and tried to guide the people in true liberation—fidelity to Yahweh. However, while Moses is on Sinai the people rebel and build a golden calf and worship it. They have forgotten what the Lord did through Moses. The Lord is ready to crush them in His anger. Moses acts as the mediator on behalf of the people. He pleads with the Lord to relent and appeals to the promises made to Abraham, Isaac and Israel. Moses reminds the Lord of the Exodus and how it was His power that liberated the Jews. Now the greatness of God's power will be revealed in His fidelity and compassion.

The Israelites in the desert are a stiff-necked people. They continually reject the Lord and the leaders He sends them. The Gospel reveals how closed people can be to God's saving action. Jesus is sent as the Savior to liberate all people from sin and death. Unfortunately, the people refuse to believe in Jesus. Instead they want to kill him. Jesus appeals to the Jewish system of justice, which accepted the testimony of two witnesses. Jesus indicates that he has such witnesses: Moses, John the Baptist, and the deeds given him to do by the Father. In spite of this, they refuse to believe, and only seek to trap Jesus in order to put him to death.

THE GOLDEN CALF

It is hard for Catholics to read the first commandment forbidding sculptured images (and this passage from the

Book of Exodus about the golden calf), and not feel uncomfortable. Much of traditional Catholic piety was (and still is) invested in statues and relics of the saints. Many of our Protestant brothers and sisters (especially in the pre-Vatican II days before we knew they were our brothers and sisters) accused us of idolatry. Of course, we explained our devotion to saints, relics and statues as symbols which helped us to keep God, or the life of the saint, in mind. We didn't really worship the statue, relic or saint. While there is the danger that such devotion may become magic, the religious value of such piety was (is) beneficial. Yet we must be on guard against idolatry and magic.

The Decalogue forbade the making of images because to do so was an attempt by humans to control the deity. The ancient peoples often associated some aspect of nature with gods. Hence, the images may represent some animal which would give one access to the divine. However, Yahweh is not like any other god. Yahweh is the Lord who proclaims, "I AM WHO I AM." The Israelites cannot relate to and control Yahweh like all the other peoples and their gods. Yahweh is different and so the Israelites must be different. Idolatry is a return to the old ways of relating to God. Yahweh cannot be controlled and manipulated. The covenant is the free, loving self-disclosure of God to Israel, with the demand that Israel respond likewise. Trust and confidence are needed, not statues and techniques for manipulation. Idolatry speaks of insecurity, and the substitution of magic for the covenant relationship.

Idolatry is the raising of the finite to the infinite, the temporal to the absolute. In our Gospel reading from John, the Jews have raised their religion and election as God's people to the level of absolute privilege. They cannot accept

Jesus, since he does not fit any of their categories or expectations. He is the reminder that no cult, code, creed or organization can replace the living God whom they are supposed to serve. We are not called to believe *in* any of these external forms, no matter how attractive or worthy. Rather, we believe *through* them as they point to the living, uncontrollable God. We can't possess God, for He is always seeking to draw us into a deeper relationship with Him. The covenant is not one of control, but of love.

Golden calves still clutter the landscape, seeking our worship. Money, the praise of others, power, intelligence, beauty, sexuality and countless other idols have their worshippers. Let us be clear that Yahweh-Jesus has ruled out idols. There is no God like the One who delivered His people from Egypt and revealed Himself on the Cross. The God we are called to worship is a gracious and loving God who freely gives Himself to us. It would certainly be easier and less demanding if Yahweh and Jesus were like other gods. Golden calves have a way of *taking* life, but they can't give it. Golden calves must be controlled and manipulated. They demand our words and a sacrifice now and then. Yahweh-Jesus speaks to us of the God who is compassionate and loving and demanding. God is totally giving, and demands we do the same.

Friday of the Fourth Week
Wisdom 2:1, 12-22
John 7:1-2, 10, 25-30

The Book of Wisdom was written around the year 50 B.C. Our reading contrasts the way of the wicked with the way of the just one. The wicked do not think with virtue, but only think their own evil thoughts. As a person thinks, so is that person. The wicked judge the just one by false standards. They set traps to see if the just one is really speaking the truth. Ultimately, the wicked will test the just one through suffering and death. They will do this to see if God comes to his aid. The just one trusts in the Lord. He is not concerned about human praise or punishment. Rather, he looks to the Lord for deliverance and healing.

Jesus is the Just One of the Father, who comes to tell the truth that sets hearts free. Jesus does not come in a loud and flashy way, but he is the Suffering Servant by whose stripes we are healed. The authorities react much as the wicked do in the Book of Wisdom. They want to kill Jesus. However, the hour for Jesus to be handed over to the powers of darkness is not yet. He must still go about making the Father's name known and doing the works of the Father—bringing salvation to all who believe. True wisdom is a gift to the one who seeks to do God's will. Jesus is the perfection of wisdom. He was sent by the Father, and will complete his mission through the Cross and resurrection.

THE HOUR

The Bible speaks to us of the mystery of time. And time is a mystery. St. Augustine once said of time: "If no one asks about time I know what it is. If someone asks me to explain it I do not know." For our Greek ancestors, time was a curse which spoke of decay and death. Modern existential philosophers speak of time in terms of the present moment and the need to make decisions. The modern scientific understanding of time is that it is the duration between successive events. We might call this mathematical or *chronos* time. It is the time of the wristwatch and the calendar. This mode of time can be quantified. However, to return to the Scriptures, the Bible speaks to us of a different mode of time. This category of time is set apart from the ones just mentioned.

The Bible speaks of the *kairos* moment of time. *Kairos* time is the time of deep and significant meaning. It is the time of decision and confrontation. Such time cannot be placed in neat categories of mathematics. We cannot quantify such time. *Kairos* time is deeply religious in the widest sense of the term. It is the encounter with the sacred or the holy. It speaks to us of the 'other dimension' of existence which we often forget or overlook in our busy world. *Kairos* time draws us out of ourselves and involves our whole being. *Kairos* time can occur as we watch a sunrise or sunset, view a work of art, read a poem, or simply walk down the street and become aware of the contingency and graciousness of life. We need not exist, yet we do and it is good.

The Scriptures are filled with *kairos* times when God displays His power and calls people to a decision. The Old Testament speaks of creation, the Exodus-Sinai experience, and the work of the prophets as times of encounter and confrontation with the Most Holy Lord. The Book of Wisdom, in our first reading, speaks of the time when the just one will be vindicated by God. It is a time of deliverance and judgment.

Nowhere is the notion of *kairos* time more important than in the Fourth Gospel. John continually speaks of 'the hour.' Again, this is not mathematical time but a judgment or decision. In the person of Jesus one is confronted with the need to make a decision for or against him in terms of belief and disbelief. The hour of Jesus is the supreme moment of revelation, when he reveals the very name—essence—of the Father. The hour for Jesus is the Cross, when he reveals the name of God as suffering, enduring love. The hour of the Cross is understood by the world to be the destruction and rejection of Jesus. However, to the eye of faith, this is the supreme moment of victory. The Light shines into the darkness of sin and death, and overcomes the forces of Satan. The exaltation of Jesus comes through the scandal of the Cross.

Lent is a *kairos* time for each of us. It is a time of confrontation and decision. Through Baptism, we are called to share in the hour of Jesus. It is through our participation in the Cross of Jesus that we have the hope of resurrection. Lent challenges us to examine how well we have kept the commitment, and followed Jesus. Our Gospel reading ends by saying that Jesus' hour had not yet come. But come it will. The hour for us is *now*, and we are called to follow Him.

Saturday of the Fourth Week
Jeremiah 11:18-20
John 7:40-53

Jeremiah, as a prophet of Yahweh, went about preaching God's word and calling the people to repentance and conversion. One gets the impression that Jeremiah expected the people to accept him and treat him with reverence. After all, he is a messenger of God! However, Jeremiah is in for a rude awakening. The people are plotting to kill him. Jeremiah sees himself as a lamb led to the slaughter. In this he is a forerunner of Christ—the Suffering Servant of Yahweh. The passage ends on a note of defiance. Jeremiah appeals to the justice of Yahweh. He asks the Lord to let him witness the destruction of those who plot against him. Only Yahweh can help him.

As Jesus goes among the people, revealing the Father, they come to believe in him. The people start to call Jesus 'the Prophet' and even 'the Messiah.' This causes the Jewish authorities to plot against Jesus, as Jeremiah was plotted against. The authorities try to use the Scriptures to 'prove' that Jesus cannot be the Messiah. The Messiah must come from Bethlehem and be of David's family. However, the learned are thrown into confusion, and no agreement is reached. Nicodemus tries to appeal to the law in order to give Jesus a fair hearing, but he is ridiculed. The authorities reject Jesus. According to them, only the ignorant and sinners accept Jesus.

THE MESSIAH

The winged chariot of time is hurrying near as we

approach the final days of Lent, and prepare to celebrate the death and resurrection of Jesus Christ. There is a sense of urgency in today's readings, as the shadow of the Cross grows more prominent. The prophet Jeremiah becomes the object of a plot to have him killed. He must say and do things which upset people's comfortable ways of living. The response at first is to either ignore the prophet or discredit him. If he persists, then he must be put to death. Jesus is also the object of much concern by the Jewish authorities, who are afraid the people will follow him and reject their teachings. Hence, they meet to draw up plans to effectively deal with this troublemaker.

As long as Jesus had few followers, and was out of public view, the authorities regarded him more as a curiosity than a threat. However, in our Gospel reading the crowd hears the words of Jesus and begins to proclaim him 'the prophet' and 'the Messiah.' This cannot be tolerated. Such talk is subversive and blasphemous. In the name of all that is holy, it must be stopped! Jesus must be silenced. Yet Nicodemus, the one who came to Jesus by night, now speaks on behalf of the true Light. Nicodemus confronts his peer group and calls them to task for their narrow and unjust ways. He reminds his colleagues that a man is innocent until proven guilty. Through slander, gossip and pride they have already condemned Jesus. The Pharisees only taunt Nicodemus, and ask if he is not a Galilean too. The Pharisees believed that the Messiah had to come out of Bethlehem and the House of David. Therefore, this disqualified Jesus. Finally, the only ones who believe that Jesus is the Messiah are the sinners, the ignorant and the outcasts of society.

The blindness of the Pharisees is evident. Jesus simply couldn't be the Messiah. He didn't fit the mold of *their* expectations. The Messiah, the Anointed One, must have the following qualifications: be of royal descent (David), be from the right part of town (Bethlehem), be surrounded by the mighty and the learned, have good social connections, and have the power to reestablish the political kingdom of Israel, which is now equivalent to God's Kingdom. Naturally, Jesus need not apply as Messiah. The Messiahship of Jesus is one which announces the good news of salvation and liberation to all people. The long reign of sin and death is over. God does not fit the expectations of humans. God expects us to respond to the new things He does. The mighty and the learned are those who are rejected by the world and the self-righteous. The Messiahship of Jesus is one of suffering and rejection. Above all, it is one of hope, for the Cross will give way to the glory of the resurrection and the newness of life.

Christian discipleship is a reminder of how much we are called by word and deed to proclaim Christ. This is not easy. Jeremiah, in the Old Testament, experienced the hostilities of others. Nicodemus has to confront the blindness of his own learned friends. He suffered ridicule and a loss of respect. In following Jesus, we can expect the same treatment. Fear not! The same Spirit who raised Jesus is with us through Baptism. It is in these daily 'deaths' that we are born to new life.

Fifth Week of Lent

Monday of the Fifth Week
Daniel 13:1-9, 15-17, 19-30, 33-62
John 8:1-11

These last sections of the Book of Daniel raise and answer one of the oldest and most troubling issues to confront the person of faith: which is stronger, virtue or vice? The story of Susanna is used to provide the answer. Susanna is a beautiful and virtuous married woman. She is falsely accused of sinful behavior. The craftiness of the wicked seems to have her caught in a no-win situation. According to the Law of Moses, she must be put to death. However, God comes to her aid, and raises up Daniel to defend her. It seems as if the evil judges have triumphed. Not so. In the end, virtue proves to be stronger than evil. God does not abandon the virtuous and leave them to be destroyed by the wicked. Daniel is a forerunner of Jesus, who is the Savior of the World.

Jesus is confronted with a woman caught in adultery. The Law of Moses demands that she be put to death. The Pharisees are anxious to see what he will do. If Jesus says to let her go, he has no respect for morals and the law. If he says to have her stoned, he would not be practicing what he preached about love and forgiveness. Jesus stuns the Pharisees by saying, "Let him who is without sin cast the first stone." The situation that was to trap Jesus has now silenced the self-righteous. Jesus pronounces the words of forgiveness and life, "Neither do I condemn you. Go and sin no more." While this story was not part of the original Gospel, it does fit perfectly the Fourth Gospel's image of God— forgiving love.

SOFT ON SIN

Several years ago, the famous psychiatrist Karl Menninger wrote a book entitled, *Whatever Became of Sin?* The book was well received in secular and religious quarters. The basic thesis of the book was as follows: we no longer talk about sin. Instead, we speak of crime and sickness. Crime is the result of a broken family or a poor socio-economic background. Psychological sickness results from poor role models, poor self image, or feelings of inferiority. In both cases, the individual is not responsible for his actions. There are external and internal causes which overpower free will, and cause one to act contrary to the law and the healthy personality. Dr. Menninger chides the priest, minister and rabbi for giving up sin-talk. Menninger believes that we must once again use the vocabulary of sin and morals, and be willing to punish those who act in an irresponsible way. Such tough talk strikes a responsive chord in the hearts of many.

As we read the story of the woman caught in adultery, and Jesus' response, we might get the idea that Jesus is soft on sin. The law is clear: a woman who commits adultery must be stoned. This woman is nothing like Susanna in the Book of Daniel. Jesus does not say that she is wrongly accused. Even the woman offers no conflicting story. Simply put: this woman is an adulteress, and the law says what must be done. So is Jesus soft? Would Dr. Menninger be disappointed in Jesus? I hope and think not. Jesus is more *demanding* than the Pharisees.

It is true that the woman is an adulteress. Neither she nor Jesus offers any excuse. Jesus pays her the highest compliment: he takes her seriously. She is not a victim, out of control, at the mercy of forces which rob her of freedom. She is responsible, and Jesus treats her responsibly. He dismisses those who are interested in death and destruction. The Pharisees will do anything and use anyone to trap Jesus. If this woman's death will achieve that end, so be it. By contrast, Jesus is the one who comes to bring life, and bring it to the full. The ministry of Jesus is to reveal the name of the Father as suffering, forgiving love. It is for the lost and alienated that Jesus came to announce the good news of acceptance and love.

Jesus treats this woman as a responsible human being who has betrayed the marriage covenant. Jesus' words reveal to her the very nature of God's covenant with His people: faithful, forgiving love. The agents of death depart, and she is left alone with Jesus. No one is left to condemn. Jesus now pronounces the words of challenge and life. He does not condemn her, but challenges her to put the past behind and go forth and live. The forgiveness of Jesus has liberated her from sin and death. She is now reborn through the loving forgiveness of Jesus. We see in this story an anticipation of the Cross and resurrection. Through Jesus' death and resurrection, sin and death are overcome. New life is offered to all who respond in faith.

Lent is the season of conversion, forgiveness and life. It is the time which challenges us to remember that the God we worship is the God of forgiving, challenging love. God does not condemn, but always seeks to redeem whatever good is present in each heart and situation. He expects His people to forgive and challenge with love, in imitation of Jesus. This isn't a sign of weakness, or that we are soft on sin. Rather, it says that Yahweh and Jesus demand more than stones of anger and self-righteousness. God demands that we acknowledge our sinfulness and turn to Him for healing. The words of Jesus are for us as well: "Neither do I condemn you. Go and sin no more."

Tuesday of the Fifth Week
Numbers 21:4-9
John 8:21-30

The essence of the covenant between Yahweh and Israel is that of fidelity. The Lord is a faithful and compassionate God. He never forgets His people, and is always mindful of their well-being. Yahweh demands that the people love Him with their whole being and keep faithful to the covenant presented by Moses. While Yahweh is always faithful, the Israelites are known to forget, chase other gods and murmur against the Lord and His leaders. In the book of Numbers, the people are growing tired of the desert and the manna. They are ungrateful, and rebel against God and Moses. The Lord sends serpents to bite the people, and many die. The people ask Moses to intercede for them. He prays and builds a bronze serpent, so that all who look at the serpent will be healed. Again we see the dynamic of disobedience, Yahweh's anger, Moses' praying on behalf of the people, and the Lord's forgiving and healing His people.

The Pharisees have been watching and planning how to trap Jesus and have him killed. Jesus predicts his death and return to the Father. The Pharisees only understand this to be a threat of suicide. The Pharisees understand at the level of the flesh. However, to the eye of faith, Jesus is speaking about the Cross and the hour of glory. The serpent was lifted up in the desert by Moses, and the people were healed. Now the Son of Man will be lifted up on the Cross in order to heal and save the whole world. Those who look at the Cross through faith will see that Jesus is I AM.

I AM

One of the important insights to be gained from Israel's religious experience is that Yahweh cannot be compared to any other god. He cannot be controlled by human expectations, and so graven images are out of order. Moses encounters Yahweh on Sinai and wants to know what he is to call this rather strange desert God. Immediately, Moses knows that this God is like no other. The Lord responds, "I AM WHO I AM." This is a divinely polite way of saying "none of your business. I AM is not answerable to you. I AM is a compassionate and loving God who wants to enter into covenant with you. But I AM does so on His terms not yours." I AM is the divine name used to express this gracious and demanding God who is like no other in all the heavens and the earth. Israel is to be a nation like no other as well.

As we approach the final showdown between Jesus and the authorities the confrontations become more tense. In our Gospel reading, Jesus speaks to the Pharisees about the workings of the Spirit and the story of salvation. They do not understand, for they judge by the standards of the flesh and their own prejudices. In the words of Jesus, "I belong to what is above. You belong to this world." Only if the Pharisees open their hearts and experience a rebirth will they be saved. If they persist in their rejection of Jesus, they "will surely die in their sins." Jesus states to them in a most dramatic way who he is. Jesus is the human form of God. Jesus is Yahweh in human form. Jesus is I AM! He has tried to tell them this all along, but in their blindness they would not be open to the Light. Jesus does not come to judge or condemn anyone. His mission is to reveal the Father, the I AM, and he will do this on the Cross.

In this appeal to the Pharisees, Jesus uses the image of the bronze serpent. As we read in the Book of Numbers, the people complained against Yahweh and Moses. Yahweh sends serpents to punish them. Many are killed. Moses intercedes on behalf of Israel, and the people are healed by looking at the serpent and believing. Jesus is in the midst of those who are just as rebellious and blind. The Pharisees will die in their sins, unless they look in faith to Jesus as I AM lifted up on the Cross. Healing from the sting of sin and death is offered to all who accept Jesus in faith. The life that Jesus is offering to all people is not that of a physical recovery, but a rebirth in spirit and truth. Jesus offers, to all who believe, the gift of eternal life. Jesus is also the New Moses who will lift himself up in love on behalf of the people on the Cross.

We can only imagine how shocked the Pharisees (maybe us as well?) must have been at the words of Jesus. He was saying that if you want to see what Yahweh is all about, then look at the Cross. In the suffering, pain, neglect, hatred, injustice, bitterness, brokenness and death see I AM. If you really want to know the name of the God of power who spoke the world into existence, liberated a people with mighty signs and wonders, raised up prophets and kings, defeated the great armies of the earth, then look to the Cross and see the One lifted up. Look at the Cross in all of its scandal and folly, and believe that there is Yahweh—I AM.

The Cross is the answer to the question Moses asked on a mountain long ago: What is your name? Who are you, so I can tell them who did such mighty deeds? I AM is Jesus on the Cross as suffering, enduring love. This we believe. Lord, help our unbelief!

Wednesday of the Fifth Week
Daniel 3:14-20, 91-92, 95
John 8:31-42

Earlier in Lent (the Tuesday of the Third Week), we read the beautiful and confident prayer of Azariah as he was put into the oven by Nebuchadnezzar. Azariah prayed to the Lord with confidence, and he was delivered. In our present reading, we are told what brought Azariah and his two friends to such a punishment. Nebuchadnezzar built a statue and ordered Shadrach, Meshach and Abednego (Azariah) to worship it. They refuse. It is the Lord alone who is deserving of worship and praise. Nebuchadnezzar has them thrown into the fire but they do not die. So great is their faith and courage that even Nebuchadnezzar praises the Lord.

The confrontation between Jesus and the Pharisees continues. The true disciple, the person of authentic faith, is the one who believes in Jesus because of his words, and not because of signs. The Pharisees appeal to their traditions and the fact that they are descendants of Abraham. Jesus tells them that the only truly free person is the one who turns from sin and believes in him as the Christ. In fact, if they were really children of Abraham they would accept and rejoice in Jesus. However, because they are blind and hard of heart, they refuse to believe. They are slaves of sin.

FREEDOM

Victor Hugo once said that there is nothing more powerful than an idea whose time has come. One such powerful idea for the modern person is freedom. The existentialist philosophers (Sartre, Camus, Heidegger, etc.) extol the importance of freedom for living the authentic life. Politicians speak constantly of our blessings of freedom, and of those totalitarian forces which seek to enslave us. Our cultural and intellectual heritage (the Enlightenment) values freedom of the mind and freedom of speech. The great universities of the world depend on academic freedom, in order that truth may be sought. Much of our talk about freedom has filtered down from these lofty perches to the person in the street, aided by commercials selling products that promise to enhance our freedom. For example, fast and sleek cars promise us the freedom of the open road. Unfortunately, some of our talk about freedom has caused us to abandon some of our most cherished commitments. In the name of freedom, we simply live together or have an "arrangement." This talk of freedom in all its aspects is not quite what Jesus had in mind. Jesus is the "truth that sets us free."

Jesus comes to speak the truth that he has received from the Father. The truth of Jesus is twofold. He is the Son of God, who has been with the Father from all eternity. Secondly, Jesus has come to tell all people that God is a loving, forgiving Father who wants to draw all people to himself. Faith is required of those who want to know the truth. The true disciple is the one who accepts the words of Jesus, and lives in a loving and compassionate way. Because we have experienced the love and forgiveness of the Father, we can love and forgive others. We are liberated from egoism and self-centeredness, which prevent us from loving God and our neighbor.

The Pharisees cannot accept Jesus as the truth of the

Father. They are only interested in their own power and self-righteousness. Jesus offers them truth, freedom and life, but they can neither accept these nor acknowledge their need for Jesus. After all, they have their laws, cultic worship and traditions. What could this carpenter's son possibly give them? Simple: the truth that will free them from their sins. The Pharisees' only response to the One who is Light and Life, is death and darkness. They plot to kill Jesus because the truth is too much for them. It does no good to appeal to Abraham. Abraham was the 'father of believers' because he trusted in God and sired a great nation. Jesus comes to call all people to faith, but the Pharisees reject him. In rejecting Jesus, they show how far from God and Abraham they really are.

In our own age, which has such a deep love affair with freedom, the words of Jesus about freedom are crucial. Too often, we understand freedom to be a negative concept. That is, we are free *from* this or that constraint. Unfortunately, it is seldom clear what we are free *for*. Jesus says that we are free *from* sin in order to be free *for* God and service to our neighbor. This freedom of Jesus is the lasting freedom of the spirit, which liberates us to live in a new way. We need no longer be imprisoned in the chains of pride, materialism, power and self-righteousness. The gifts of freedom and truth, which Jesus offers, come to all who believe in him as the Son of God. Through faith in Jesus, we have a permanent place in God's family.

The freedom that Jesus gives us through Baptism, and nourishes in the Eucharist, is one that calls us to responsibility in our daily living. We have been liberated in order to meet the needs of our neighbor. Unlike the Pharisees, who saw their relationship with Abraham as a sign of privilege, our faith relationship with Jesus is the call to greater love, service and sacrifice. True Christian freedom is always a freedom for God and the other. To be free in Christ is to know how to love and serve. Real freedom always speaks of commitment. God committed Himself to our condition and our world through the Incarnation. Jesus, in freedom and love, committed himself to the world's salvation through the Cross and resurrection. This is the truth that forgives our sins and sets us free.

Thursday of the Fifth Week
Genesis 17:3-9
John 8:51-59

In one of the most dramatic passages in all of Scripture, we witness the establishment of God's covenant with Abram. Abram is to become the father of many nations. He will now be called Abraham, for he is a new person. Abraham has a new relationship with God, and through the covenant relationship the many nations of the earth will receive a blessing. The expectations of the covenant are clear: Yahweh will be the God of Abraham and his descendants, and will give them the land of Canaan. On the part of the people, they must keep the covenant and remain faithful to the Lord. The basis of the covenant is fidelity and trust.

The Gospel of John continues the themes of promise and covenant. God is faithful, and does not forget His word. The Father sends Jesus to bring the covenant to perfection. The perfection of the covenant is established through Jesus and the Cross. The promise to Abraham was to make of him a great nation, through which all would be blessed. Now, in Jesus, this is a reality. Through the new covenant of love, Jesus draws all people to himself to be healed. The Pharisees continue to interpret Jesus' words on the level of the flesh. Jesus is not even fifty years old. How could he see Abraham? Before Abraham came to be, Jesus was. The Pharisees throw stones at him, since he is claiming to be I AM—God.

PROMISES, PROMISES

One of the prominent features of the modern scene is the loss of permanence. Things just don't seem to last as long. It's hard to find the Good Housekeeping Seal of Approval on many of our modern gadgets. Guarantees last about as long as the morning fog or dew. Not only things, but relationships don't seem to endure. There is a loss of permanence among those who say 'I do.' The divorce rate is running about even with the success rate (although many of these marriages are anything but successful). People seem to float in and out of our lives. "Brief encounters of the most superficial kind" might well describe the majority of our relationships. Things, relationships and vows seem to have little binding power. Promises made are not always promises kept. We have come to view the person as an entity in process and constant change. Hence, if I make a promise on a certain day, and I am a different person tomorrow or next week, then the promise or vow is not binding on the new me. All in all, the effect on trust and faith is devastating. How do I know the agreement made today will be honored tomorrow? The answer is simple: I don't know. Therefore I must be constantly vigilant, and suspicious of everyone. Everyone I encounter has the potential of "ripping me off." In effect, we have witnessed the rise of a modern Hobbesian version of "the war of all against all."

The question arises whether we can trust and believe in anyone or anything. Both of our readings say that we can. We can trust and have absolute faith in Yahweh and Jesus. In our first reading, Yahweh establishes His covenant with Abram. The covenant is one of life, and brings forth new life. However, Yahweh is the Lord of life, and brings forth new life where there is no hope. Yahweh is a God of surprises, and He fits no mold (hence make no statues of Him). He is not some distant, aloof despot, but a God who wants to be in relationship with His creation. He is the God of covenant relationships, and He is like no other god. Not only does Yahweh enter covenant relationship, He is also faithful without exception. Yahweh never forgets His word and His people. No matter how unfaithful Israel is, Yahweh is always faithful. Finally, He is a jealous God who demands His people's total commitment to Him. There is no such thing as a trial-covenant. Covenant demands a total giving.

The coming of Jesus is the proof that Yahweh is faithful, and can be trusted to keep His word. Yahweh promised Abraham that from his descendants would come the savior. Jesus is the Savior of the world, who comes to free all people from the slavery of sin and death. Jesus comes to establish the new covenant of love, which is now open to all people who accept him in faith as the Messiah. Even though Israel has been unfaithful many times, Yahweh will never turn away and forget what was begun with Abraham. Abraham rejoices to see the day of Jesus, for Jesus is now the One who will bring all things to completion by the Cross and resurrection. The covenant with Abraham is completed in the sacrifice of Jesus. Yahweh is faithful.

In a cynical, untrusting world, the covenant of Yahweh and Jesus has two very important things to say to us. First, Yahweh is a God who is faithful and cares about us. The God who made Himself known at Sinai and Golgotha is the God of passionate, suffering love. This is no cold and uncaring God. Our God wants what is best for each of us, and labors mightily with and for us. No matter how many times we stray, chase idols and forget God, He never forgets us.

Second, God expects us to be faithful and caring when we deal with Him and each other. Covenant is a two-way street. As God has done for us, we are to do to Him and each other. We cannot be satisfied with only receiving, or by being chased by God. We must also seek God and serve our neighbors.

As we said in the beginning, Yahweh is no ordinary God. He is faithful, loving and demanding. Sometimes it might be easier if Yahweh and Jesus had kept their distances. Why can't God just leave us alone? But if He did so, Yahweh wouldn't be Yahweh, and we would not be His people.

Friday of the Fifth Week
Jeremiah 20:10-13
John 10:31-42

No one likes to be the bearer of bad news. Such is the task of the prophet Jeremiah. Naturally, this is not welcomed and neither is Jeremiah. The people are plotting against him and planning to kill him. Perhaps the most bitter part of Jeremiah's situation is the rejection by his friends. They, too, want to trap him. Jeremiah realizes that he has only one friend and champion—the Lord. The Lord will not forsake him. The Lord knows whose heart is worthy of trust. All those who turn against the Lord will be put to shame and confusion. The passage ends on a high note of confidence, "He has rescued the life of the poor from the power of the wicked!"

Jeremiah comes to announce God's word, and is rejected. Jesus is the Word made flesh, who comes to do the Father's will. He is also rejected by the hostile Jewish authorities. The charge brought against him is that of blasphemy. Jesus is claiming to be God. The law demands death. How ironic! The One who came to give life in abundance is not only rejected, but condemned to die by the law. The totally innocent One is found guilty and condemned to die. However, through his death and resurrection, Jesus will give eternal life and resurrection to all who believe.

GOOD WORK

Humankind has experienced a love/hate relationship with work. During some periods, work was considered a bad four-letter word. At other times, it has enjoyed a privileged status. Work has been considered as a duty, a way to curb sin and idleness, and as the best expression of the human spirit. Work has made its way into various ethical theories about a just wage for a just day's labor. Perhaps the most influential view of work in recent times has been advanced by the sociologist Max Weber. Weber used his theory of the work ethic to explain the material success of Western societies (especially America). Christians were called to take care of *this* world and live a thrifty, simple life. Hence they became rich. In order to legitimize this wealth, God was seen as rewarding those who were obedient to the covenant. Finally, Pope John Paul II wrote a most sensitive and balanced encyclical on labor, entitled *On Human Work*.

With all this in mind, we should not be too surprised that Jesus is in trouble over the work he is doing, a work that greatly upsets the Pharisees. The Jews are ready to stone Jesus, so he asks, "For which of my many good deeds are you going to stone me?" They respond that it is not for good works (Jesus couldn't possibly do any good work!) but for blasphemy—claiming to be God. Yet this is the essence of Jesus' good work—to reveal the Father's name, and invite all people to true faith. The work given by the Father to Jesus is to reveal the Father's love for all people. Jesus challenges the Pharisees to faith. If he does not perform the work of God, then don't believe in him. If Jesus does the Father's work of saving, loving, healing and giving life, then believe in him. The Pharisees will not believe in Jesus, because their hearts are closed to this revelation. However, all is not lost, since many people do come to believe in Jesus. He indicates that true faith is present when one accepts him as the Christ because of his words. However, there is an imperfect form of faith that looks for signs, which is better than unbelief.

Throughout his earthly ministry, Jesus continually reminds his audience that he does not come to do his will or speak his words. Rather, he has been sent by the Father to speak His message of life and love. Through our Baptism, we are called to continue the good work of Jesus. That is, we are called to continue to reveal the Father's name as LOVE. For Jesus, through the Cross, reveals God as suffering, faithful love. When Jesus gathers with his disciples at the Last Supper, he tells them to serve one another (Washing of the Feet), and to love one another in imitation of him. Jesus expects that those who are his disciples will continue the good work of speaking God's word and doing His will.

As we live our Baptismal commitment to the work of Jesus, we should expect our share of suffering, rejections and crosses. The prophet Jeremiah finds out quickly that the work of preaching God's word can be dangerous and bitter. It may even require that we forsake some of our relationships. Some of our most trusted friends may soon reject us. However, we should never feel abandoned or alone. The Holy Spirit lives within us for courage and wisdom. Even in his moment of distress, Jeremiah turns with confidence to the Lord. He raises his voice in song and praise to the Lord who is faithful. In our own daily struggle to continue the good work of Jesus, let us show the same confidence. Let us lift up our voices in song and praise to the Lord who rescues the life of the poor.

Maybe Jeremiah is saying that song and praise, even in the most unlikely moments and seasons, are the real good works that we are called to complete.

Saturday of the Fifth Week
Ezekiel 37:21-28
John 11:45-57

What a magnificent vision offered by Ezekiel! The Israelites will be united into one nation and returned to the land of the promise. The tragic division of Israel into two kingdoms, Israel in the north and Judah in the south, will be healed. Israel shall be a nation set upon a hill, as a guide to the nations. She will return to the covenant, and be faithful to the Lord. The unified Israel will be ruled by the new David anointed by the Lord. There will not only be a political unity of north and south, but a spiritual, covenant unity grounded in fidelity to Yahweh. The Lord will be her 'ultimate concern,' and no longer will she run after false gods. All of the nations will look to Israel for guidance, for the Lord establishes an eternal and fruitful covenant of peace.

Our Gospel reading follows the raising of Lazarus. Many of the Jews believe in Jesus, while others report him to the Pharisees. The Jewish officials meet to decide what to do with Jesus. In an ironic statement, they indicate that "the whole world will believe in him." In fact, through the death and resurrection of Jesus, the gospel will be carried to the whole world by those who believe.

The raising of Lazarus is the last of the seven signs, and the one that seals Jesus' fate—he must die! The one who gave life to Lazarus is now the quarry of the forces of death. But through Jesus' death all people will be drawn to salvation.

THE COVENANT OF PEACE

Former Egyptian President Anwar Sadat once said, "one day we will learn that it takes more courage to wage peace than war." He said this after he landed in Israel to talk peace with his sworn enemies. The bitter memories of war and death in 1967 and 1973 were still in his mind: blood spilled, life destroyed, land ruined, and young men and women who would never dream dreams or see visions. Another way had to be found; a way which spoke of life and not death, peace and not war. His persistent and courageous drive for peace led him to come to the land of his enemies, and dare to make them his friends. In that one bold move, President Sadat brought the vision of Ezekiel a little closer to reality. Ezekiel's vision would be realized by the nations of the earth trying to live in justice and peace, and responding to that which unites them. President Sadat paid the ultimate price—his life—for his courage to wage peace. We are reminded that peace never comes at a cheap price. Peace demands our most creative and courageous instincts to respond to God's grace for unity.

The prophet Ezekiel is speaking to a people who are divided, broken and in strife. What they need is what most seems beyond their grasp—peace. Hence, peace is the covenant gift of Yahweh. God's peace is not something we establish, earn or impose. It is not something we can receive through the world's agenda and values, nor does it come with any particular political or social arrangement. God's peace is a pure gift of love to those who are most in need. The covenant of peace comes to those who allow God to be the center of their individual and national life. The nation that seeks after the holy will of God is the one that will find His peace. The nation which makes welcome the stranger, alien, orphan, unborn and poor is one which knows the peace of Yahweh. If it lives according to the justice of God's laws and statutes, it will be a nation fruitful and pleasing to God. Such a nation will be blessed by God. The peace of Yahweh is one which calls all the nations to reconciliation and unity, as the one family of God. The nation of God's covenant of peace is one which seeks out its enemies and makes them into friends.

Jesus came to call all people to God's covenant of peace. The power of sin and death, which keeps us enemies of God and one another, is about to end. On the Cross and through the resurrection, Jesus brings to us the peace the world cannot give and cannot take away. To believe in Jesus is to be open to receive His first post-resurrectional gift— 'peace be with you.' It does not come at an easy price. The peace that Jesus establishes comes after he endures hostility, bitterness, rejection and death at the hands of the world. To be part of the covenant of peace is to drink the cup, embrace the cross, and be baptized with the fire that transforms hearts of stone to flesh, and enemies to friends.

Lent is a season of healing, binding up old wounds, doing new things, and turning our enemies into friends. All of this is risky business. We can be fooled, abused, disappointed and even killed. But since when has following Jesus been easy and safe? Lent is a good time to remember and experience the covenant of peace, and work to extend the gift. The peace of Jesus, that has been poured into our hearts, is to be poured out into our everyday world and relationships. We are to co-labor with the Spirit for the unity that binds us into a people who seek after the justice of the Lord.

Lent is the time when we must venture forth from the security of the well-traveled path. We must go down the less-traveled road of the One who is the way, truth, life and peace. At the end of this road lies not the Emerald City and the Wizard of Oz, but the New Jerusalem and Yahweh's covenant of peace.

Holy Week

Monday of Holy Week
Isaiah 42:1-7
John 12:1-11

Our reading from Isaiah is the first of the four Servant Songs of Yahweh (49:1-6; 50:4-9; and 52:13-53:12). Yahweh is the one who speaks, and who will raise up a servant to announce judgment and righteousness to the whole earth. The servant of Yahweh is chosen by Him and filled with His spirit. The servant completes the vocation, not by loud voice or by great signs, but through fidelity to the covenant. Through this fidelity, all the nations shall be called to Yahweh's covenant of justice. Israel is the Lord's servant through whom peace and liberation will be established.

Jesus has raised Lazarus from the dead, and the Pharisees decide that he must die. Jesus withdraws to Bethany to share a meal with Mary, Martha, Lazarus, and Judas and the other disciples. Mary performs the prophetic act of anointing Jesus' feet in anticipation of his burial. Judas objects to this extravagance. The money could have been given to the poor. However, Jesus says that he is about to be taken away through his passion. Our reading ends with the statement that many of the Jews believed in Jesus because of the raising of Lazarus. The authorities decide to kill Lazarus as well. Jesus comes to give life, while the rulers of this world and their agents can only respond with darkness and death.

TABLE FELLOWSHIP

How do we find out what people are really like? How can we tell if a person is honest or dishonest; kind or cruel;

compassionate or unfeeling? The contemporary answer swings between the social sciences and the reading of the stars. A psychological test or an analysis of their home environment would provide a clue as to what a person is all about. Others would suggest reading the zodiac as a sure-fire way to get beneath the other person, and find out what makes them tick. With all due respect, the Bible suggests a different way: prepare a meal and invite people to come. If you really want to know what's going on with another person, have them break bread, and listen to what they say and *don't* say. Watch how they act and *don't* act. The Bible is saying that a meal is more than a biological necessity. Meals are sacramental—that is, they reveal the true identity of those who partake. Perhaps we know so little about our children or even our spouse, because we spend so little time eating with one another. Fast foods and rotating schedules have turned our homes into a house full of strangers. To sit down and have a meal is risky business. Not only do we find out about others, but they find out about us.

In our Gospel reading, which takes place six days before Passover, Jesus draws close to those whom he loves, for a meal. Meals have gotten Jesus in trouble before. He has had table fellowship with sinners, tax collectors, and all the wrong kinds of people. Now Jesus is having a meal with his friends, some for the last time. This meal reveals a great deal about those gathered to eat. Mary is wonderful in her extravagance and love for the Lord. She is the example of the true disciple who holds nothing back from Jesus. Martha is still Martha. She is preparing and serving the food (might she also be complaining that no one is helping her?). We see a hint of the true Judas who will betray Jesus. He pretends to be concerned for the poor, but his real concern is money. He resents Mary, for she has done what he cannot do—give and not count the cost. Lazarus is strangely silent, although the Gospel says that he will be killed as a follower of Jesus. Perhaps the best insight is reserved for Jesus.

Throughout the Fourth Gospel, Jesus is presented in a very exalted and majestic way. He is in control of every situation, and knows all that will happen. We see very little of the humanity of Jesus that is present in the Gospel of Mark. But in this table setting, his humanity peeks through. When Judas complains that Mary is wasting the ointment on him, Jesus responds, "Leave her alone. Let her keep it against the day they prepare me for burial. The poor you will always have with you, but me you will not always have." We see Jesus, the Lamb of God, the Messiah and Christ, the Anointed Servant, wanting and needing a little human concern and care. Jesus who has loved and offered acceptance to so many, now needs the warmth and support of his community of friends. Jesus who has been so generous and extravagant in anointing others with the oil of gladness, now wants to be anointed as well. He seems to be indicating that even the Messiah needs love and concern, as he prepares to face the hour for which he came into the world.

Jesus is saying to us that no one is exempt from needing love, support and intimacy. He is showing us how important it is to let others minister to us in our need. At times we can be great at giving, but not so great at giving others the opportunity to give to us. Christian spirituality is basically one in which we grow weak so that God can be strong. As long as we hold on to our illusions of control, power and self-sufficiency there is no room for the Spirit. It is only in the poverty of our condition that God can be rich in and for us. Jesus wanted and needed to have Mary minister to him. Mary needed to do this for Jesus.

This little banquet at Bethany reveals a great deal to us about Jesus and what is required to follow him. We continue the table fellowship and banquet gathering in the Eucharist. We come to the Lord's table not because of our achievements, perfections or merits, but because we are in need of nourishment. We need the support, love and intimacy of fellow believers. We need to give the same to others. During this Holy Week, our Eucharist takes on a special significance. We are being nourished against the day of his burial. We are being filled with the hope that we will come to share the glory of the resurrection.

Tuesday of Holy Week
Isaiah 49:1-6
John 13:21-33, 36-38

Isaiah presents the second of the Servant Songs. In the first song (42:1-7) the Servant is Israel. In this Song, the Servant is a specific person (Jeremiah?). The vocation of the Servant is to proclaim God's word to all people. He is in intimate relationship with Yahweh. At first, his deeds seem to amount to nothing. But the lasting reward is offered by the Lord, who makes fruitful that which seemed barren. The Servant first brings his message to Israel as the people of promise. Then his message is to be proclaimed to the whole world. The Servant is to call all people to worship Yahweh.

Our Gospel reading takes us to the Last Supper. Jesus becomes troubled over his impending passion and death. However, what disturbs Jesus immediately is the betrayal and denial by two of his disciples. Judas will hand him over for thirty pieces of silver. Jesus offers Judas the food dipped in the dish as a last chance to repent. Judas refuses, and goes off into the night. Peter proclaims that he will remain faithful to the Lord even to the point of death. However, Jesus tells Peter that before the night is over he will deny Jesus three times.

Connecting Judas' betrayal and Peter's denial is the declaration by Jesus that 'the Son of Man is glorified.' The hour is at hand, and the forces of darkness must be confronted. The disciples are not to fear, for Jesus will be glorified.

IT WAS NIGHT

Part of the American Dream is to retire after a career of long and faithful service to the company. We are surrounded by our family, friends and co-workers all wishing us well. Armed with the gold watch, we spend our remaining years in peace and integrity. We plan on doing all those things we never had a chance to do because of work. Now we will live the life of leisure in the golden age of our life. The words of the poet Robert Browning come to mind: "Grow old along with me! The best is yet to be, The last of life, for which the first was made." Naturally, this is a highly idealized picture of retirement, and many never experience it. This is certainly true in the case of Jesus. In our Gospel reading, St. John allows us to view Jesus, at the end of his mission, with his disciples.

The public ministry of Jesus is conducted in the presence of a hostile audience. In this last, holy week Jesus is now with his own, whom he loves to the end—to death. The hostility and violence of the world were expected. But even in the intimate setting of this last meal, the forces of darkness are near at hand. St. John tells us that Jesus grew deeply troubled. Among those with whom he has lived, suffered and shared the love of the Father, one will betray him and another will deny him. The Synoptic Gospels tell us that the other ten fled and left him alone. Jesus is suffering, forgiving love to the very end. He offers Judas the first morsel of food as an offering of reconciliation and peace. But Judas is too much a part of the world. He is an agent of the night, and the Light only blinds him. Hence, Judas goes out into the night to do what he must. The forces of darkness are growing more powerful, and will even grasp the Rock! Peter tells Jesus that he will follow him even if it demands his life. Jesus brings Peter back to reality. He will deny Jesus three times.

Yet even in the midst of the darkness of this night, we see the Light already shining. The prophet Isaiah, in our first reading, says that the Servant of Yahweh appears to be a failure, but that it is only an apparent failure. Through God's grace, salvation is announced to the world. So it is with Jesus. The betrayal of Jesus, his denial by Peter, and the Cross all appear to be signs of failure and God's punishment. But to the eye of faith this is the hidden victory, illuminated through belief. St. John tells us that when Judas goes into the night, the process of Jesus' glorification begins. For the Cross is the hour of glory, even though Jesus seems most weak, helpless and forsaken. The Cross reveals the true nature of God as suffering love. It is through the Cross that salvation will come to the whole world. The new covenant in Jesus is now established for all who believe and love.

At times we may wonder about Judas and Peter. How could they do what they did? How could Judas betray Jesus for money? How could Peter disown his Lord? Yet if we are honest, we know well the doings of Judas and Peter. Our betrayals and denials are just more subtle and banal. We often betray Jesus by our failure to seek him with all our heart. We compromise the gospel in the name of worldly realism. By not loving our neighbor and making our enemy a friend, we disown the One who came to make all of us brothers and sisters.

Our betrayals and denials of Jesus should not cause us to despair. Rather, we see in Jesus the constant offer to reconciliation and life. Judas is offered the morsel as a sign that

Jesus desires for him to be saved. Peter will turn from this moment of weakness, and become a good shepherd who will lay down his life for Christ. Jesus is always ready to welcome us back to the table. While there are some dark nights ahead for Jesus, let us not lose heart. For in the midst of the night, the One who is Light and Life will not be overcome.

Wednesday of Holy Week
Isaiah 50:4-9
Matthew 26:14-25

The third of the Servant Songs reveals to us another aspect of the Servant of Yahweh. He must suffer. Suffering is related to the vocation of preaching God's word. The Servant has been given the gift of speech, so that he might call the people to conversion and a change of heart. Each day the Servant is ready to listen, and do what the Lord requires of him. He is obedient, and never rejects the mission to preach, even though rejection and suffering are involved. The anger of the people is not met with violence, but with resignation and trust in the Lord. Suffering is not a sign of God's punishment or disapproval. In the end, the Lord will rescue and redeem His servant. If people judge Yahweh's Servant to be guilty, let them appear before Yahweh who judges justly. The Servant Song ends on a note of vindication and hope: "See, the Lord is my help."

Jesus is the true and perfect Servant of Yahweh. He suffers in silence, and he is totally innocent. Jesus has proclaimed the Kingdom, healed the sick, raised the dead, forgiven sins, and called those who were far off to return to the peace of God. Now in these final days, Jesus experiences betrayal, denials, rejection, suffering and death. The world understands the Cross as the failure of Jesus, and the rejection by God of all that Jesus did and said. However, to those who see with the eye of faith, the Cross is the 'power to save.' It is through the Cross that Jesus will be vindicated and raised on the third day. The resurrection is God's statement that Jesus is Lord.

SUFFERING LOVE

What a strange combination of words—suffering and love. They seem to be mutually exclusive. Suffering speaks of evil, punishment, broken bodies, and anguished cries in the night for help. Suffering evokes in us (who are so comfort-oriented) a good deal of 'negative vibes.' All in all, it is not one of our favorite topics. By contrast, love is the essence of everything that is pleasing and attractive. Love brings us peace and a sense of well-being. It speaks of wholeness and an inner contentment which is hard to describe. Hence, the connection of love with suffering seems very much out of place. To the contemporary, perhaps. However, the Bible advances the notion that we cannot know true love without suffering. They are intimately related.

Just what do we mean by suffering? Naturally, there is a suffering filled with anguish, which eventually destroys the body and spirit. There is the suffering that is non-redemptive and anti-life. Wars, poverty, violence and disease are negative, and should be fought against. The Bible speaks of a time for healing and binding up old wounds, as well as of the glory of the resurrection. Yet there is another meaning of suffering (*pathos*). Suffering is the ability to be moved to respond. It is the power to get involved, and become concerned about a person or event. Suffering is a sign that we are alive and capable of loving. The Bible speaks of Yahweh's sufferings for and with His people. The covenant is proof that God gets involved with and cares about Israel. Yahweh is laboring with His people during their slavery, exodus, desert wanderings and final entrance into Canaan. He suffers with Israel throughout their history, as they go back and forth between fidelity and idolatry. The ultimate proof of God's suffering is the sending of the Son into our human condition and history. The Word became flesh because God is Love, and cannot help but get involved with His creation. The God who is Love is also the God who suffers, labors and cares for us.

The Sinai covenant and the Incarnation say to us that we cannot have love at a distance, free of all the sufferings, confusions, betrayals and crosses that are part of the human condition. Yahweh did not enter into covenant with Israel at a distance. He became involved in their history, problems, possibilities, hopes, dreams, failures and successes. Yahweh was their God, and they were to be His people, in a relationship of suffering love. The Incarnation reveals just how much God loves us and is involved with us. God became human, and revealed the essential aspects of human history and life. In Jesus, we see how much God has labored and suffered to reveal the meaning of life and history: love, fidelity and community.

During Holy Week, we see clearly the connection between suffering and love. The Last Supper, the Passion, and the Cross speak to us of the meaning of suffering as care, love, involvement and commitment. Holy Week also speaks to us of the redemptive value of suffering love in creating new life. Holy Week leads to the first day of the week, and the beginning of new life. The suffering love of the Cross turns into the hope of resurrection.

Holy Thursday
Exodus 12:1-8, 11-14
1 Cor 11:23-26
John 13:1-15

Our first reading, from the Book of Exodus, presents the Passover meal. The Passover meal is connected with the deliverance of the Israelites from slavery in Egypt. It was the memorial of the Exodus—the greatest of the mighty acts of God on behalf of His people. The Passover meal is to be eaten as if one is in flight. Every time the Israelites gather to eat it, they remember and reexperience Yahweh's mighty care. The night of the Passover meal is different from all others, because on this night God saved His people.

St. Paul, in his first letter to the Corinthians, narrates the new and perfect Passover. Jesus is the perfect Lamb who takes away the sins of the world by his sacrificial death on the Cross. The Eucharist is our food for this life and for eternal life. Every time we gather to share the cup and break the bread, we remember the death and resurrection of Jesus until he comes in full glory.

In order to properly participate in the Eucharist, we must live a life of humble service and love. This life of service is made possible by the Eucharist. Jesus gives the example for his disciples, that they must serve and love one another. Greatness and authority are invitations to serve and not be served. The Christian must integrate both Eucharist and community service in order to achieve a full spiritual life.

AN EXAMPLE

All of us have had the experience of being in school, and not grasping the lesson being taught. For most of us, it was probably math or science. Things seemed so abstract and disconnected from our everyday lives. We felt that the lesson was important and needed to be learned, but that it was beyond our poor capacity. If the teacher was conscientious, he or she probably tried to help with an abundance of examples. Maybe these lofty principles and complex teachings would make sense if we could grasp an example. Maybe the teacher could relate the lesson to my life, by some word or action which would give 'real' meaning to the lesson. Often, examples help to make concrete and specific the most abstract and sublime teachings.

Jesus gathers his disciples, who are now friends, for a last meal. He has told them so much, and revealed so much of the Father's loving will to them. Essentially, Jesus wanted them to know how much God loved them and wanted to share His life with them. Jesus wanted them to be a community of fraternal love, and thereby share the same love with each other. Pretty heady stuff! They often misunderstood and disobeyed the vision of Jesus. At this last meal, Jesus gives them an example of all that he tried to teach during his earthly ministry. Jesus performs 'a parable in action' (Fr. Bruce Vawter, C.M.), in which he shows them in a specific and concrete and shocking way what it means to be a disciple. In so doing, he also shows them how he, Lord and God, sees his teaching ministry. Jesus washes their feet, and tells them to do the same if they want to have communion with him. Why did he do such a thing?

The Gospel of St. Luke (chapter 22:24-30) provides an

insight. The disciples had been arguing about who was the greatest among them, so that when Jesus leaves this greatest can be in authority. Jesus could have preached many fine sermons, or even told them a story or parable. He went beyond all that. He gave them an example of what it means to be the greatest—wash feet. If you want to be first, then learn to wash feet: be last, serve and learn from all. The attitude and actions of Jesus must become part of your life. If not, you can have no part with him.

The disciples still do not understand what Jesus did and said. That will only come later with the sending of the Holy Spirit. The Church, and each of us, still struggles to really understand what Jesus was about. Every time we grasp for power and privilege, we have no part in Jesus. It is only through our willingness to be the humble servant of all, that we have communion with Jesus. It is only in giving up rank and power that we become truly strong, by allowing the Spirit to work through us.

The example that Jesus gives is crucial, yet a hard one to learn. Maybe it would have been better if Jesus had just told us about service and love, rather than showed us. It certainly would have been easier if Jesus had written a book or given us some high spirituality. Then we could claim that we never read the book, or that we didn't understand what he meant. But no. Jesus goes and does something we can't get around. He washes their feet, and tells us to do likewise so that we can be his disciples.

Finally, the washing of feet calls to mind our baptismal commitment to be part of Jesus and the new creation. Water is an eschatological symbol of God's Kingdom and the Messianic age. To be part of the Kingdom, and live in the new age, requires that we live in a new way. The agenda and values of the world are transformed into new ways of relating and living. We no longer lord it over others, but pour ourselves out in humble service. On this Holy Thursday night let us pray that, as Jesus was an example, we too might be examples of his abiding love and service.

Good Friday
Isaiah 52:13-53:12
Hebrews 4:14-16; 5:7-9
John 18:1-19:42

The last of the Servant Songs clearly presents the Servant as one who suffers innocently, and then is exalted by the Lord. The Suffering Servant comes from humble origins, and grows up to serve the Lord completely. He is familiar with suffering and rejection. Many believe that this is God's rejection of the Servant. However, suffering and rejection are part of God's mysterious plan for salvation. The Servant suffers innocently and is put to death. But the Lord raises the Servant, and through his suffering many are healed. It is easy to see how the New Testament writers and the Church so identified Jesus with the Suffering Servant.

The Letter to the Hebrews presents Jesus as the great high priest. Jesus offers the perfect sacrifice—freely offering himself for sin. Our high priest, Jesus, is one who knows what it is to be human and to suffer. Hence, we can come to God with our problems and infirmities, since Jesus is well acquainted with the human condition. Above all, he came as the obedient Son who suffered and died on our behalf. By so doing, Jesus won eternal salvation for all who obey the loving will of the Father.

The Passion according to St. John is filled with the majesty and divine authority of Jesus. While the world understands the Cross as a scandal and as a rejection of Jesus, to the eye of faith it is the hour of glory. It is the moment of Jesus' supreme victory over the powers of *darkness. He is the true King of the Jews and the Savior of the whole world. The power and majesty of Jesus is that of suffering, faithful love.*

THE SCANDAL OF DEATH

We are all aware of the saying, 'familiarity breeds contempt.' Familiarity also breeds the illusion that we know someone or something completely. Familiarity can take the most profound of experiences, and reduce it to the ordinary, taken-for-granted, and unappreciated. Familiarity leads us to believe wrongly that we have nothing further to learn. It turns into contempt, or worse, apathy. The familiar simply fails to move, inspire and provide guidance for life. In New Orleans, there is the Superdome. We have termed it the 'eighth wonder of the world.' When I first entered 'the Dome,' I was deeply moved by its size and human achievement. Now I hardly take notice, as I rush to my seat. So much for 'the eighth wonder of the world.'

Familiarity and its destructive ability to leave us apathetic, affects much of religion. We can listen to the most sublime mysteries of God and human existence, yet remain unaffected. Our response to the parables of Jesus is often, "I've heard that before. Isn't there anything new?" The familiarity that breeds apathy even finds its way into Holy Week and Good Friday. Each year, we come to remember the death of Jesus. We take part in the Way of the Cross. We may even venerate it with a kiss. Yet this day has become too familiar to us. It is too predictable and comfortable. Jesus died. Jesus went into the tomb. Jesus rose. And our life goes on. If this day, and what we have done these past forty days, is to have real meaning, we must confront the scandal of this day. We must experience its shock and the horror.

In the earthly ministry of Jesus, the idea of a Messiah who must suffer, be rejected and die, was deeply troubling to the disciples. Peter tried to tell Jesus to avoid Jerusalem. The expectations of the Jewish people for the Messiah were very different from what they found in Jesus. The Messiah should be one of power and glory. He would establish God's reign, and liberate Israel from foreign occupation. The glory of King David would return. However, in Jesus these expectations were not realized. Jesus is the Messiah who is the Suffering Servant of Yahweh. He cannot heed the advice of Peter (who is really speaking like Satan!), for his destiny is to drink the cup the Father has given him. The early Church had to confront proclaiming Jesus as both the Son of God and the Crucified One. Down to this very day, the passion and death of Jesus continues to be a scandal, a stumbling block, a folly to the world which looks at the Cross with disbelief and repugnance.

This day challenges us to take part in the scandal of death and of the Cross. Whenever death comes, it is always unexpected, unwelcomed and raged against. Why are we born to die? Our first breath is the first movement toward death. Life is so precious and filled with opportunities. What a waste and an insult! Death is the absurdity of life. How much more for *this* man on *this* day in *this* way? Jesus was a man sent by God to announce the good news of salvation. He offered sight to the blind, freedom to those in bondage. He said that the lame would walk and the poor would share in the Lord's year of favor. Unfortunately, the authorities found this good news, bad news. The self-righteous and the smug took offense at the ease with which Jesus spoke of God and invited others to do so. The response of the world to this man of good news was the Cross. On this day, this man died this way. We must come to terms not only with the scandal of death, but with the scandal of the shameful death on the Cross.

On this Good Friday, let us resist the temptation to rush to Easter and the words 'he is risen!'. Let us this day stay with the scandal of this man's death on the Cross. Let us resist the easy way out of looking past the Cross to the empty tomb. Let us confront the challege that the Cross holds for every Christian—here is God, and here is the way to fellowship with Him. Today, let us stay with the closing words of St. John's account of the Passion, "They buried Jesus there, for the tomb was close at hand."

Holy Saturday (Vigil)

1. Genesis 1:1—2:2

   The opening of Genesis recounts the power of God's creative word. God speaks the world into existence. The crown of creation is the bringing forth of the human person. The dignity of the person comes from being made in God's image and likeness. God pronounces the creation very good.

2. Genesis 22:1-18

   God established His covenant with Abraham, and promised to make him a great nation and a blessing to all people. Now God requires that Abraham sacrifice Isaac. In a great act of faith, Abraham prepares to do what the Lord requires. God does not allow him to carry the deed through. In the fullness of time, God will send His own Son, Jesus.

3. Exodus 14:15—15:1

   In this passage, the greatest event in Israel's history is told. Israel is liberated from Egypt by the mighty arm of Yahweh. God is involved with the history of Israel, and leads her through the Red Sea. Through the death and resurrection of Jesus, we are freed from sin and death.

4. Isaiah 54:5-14

   Fidelity is the essential aspect of the covenant between Yahweh and Israel. While Yahweh is always faithful, Israel often breaks the covenant. Yahweh abandons Israel for a little while, so that she may come to her senses. But ultimately Yahweh is faithful, and His love shall never leave her.

5. Isaiah 55:1-11

   God's covenant and love for Israel is a free gift. Yahweh

calls for all the people to turn from sin, and come back
to Him. To be in covenant relationship with Yahweh is
to live and be fruitful. Yahweh is filled with compassion
and forgiveness for His people.

6. Baruch 3:9-15, 32—4:4

   *Baruch calls Israel to keep the Lord's commandments.
   Israel is captive in a foreign land because she has
   broken the new covenant. She has forsaken wisdom,
   prudence and knowledge, and hence knows no peace.
   Israel's only hope is to return to the Lord and be healed.
   Israel is blessed since she has been given the Law.*

7. Ezekiel 36:16-28

   *Israel has forsaken the covenant, and gone over to idol
   worship. The holy name of Yahweh has been defiled by
   Israel's unfaithfulness. God's power will be shown
   when He gathers Israel back to the land and the covenant. Yahweh will replace her stony heart with a heart
   directed to the Lord.*

8. Romans 6:3-11 (Epistle)

   *St. Paul reminds us that our baptism is a sharing in the
   death and resurrection of the Lord Jesus. By being
   united with Christ, we die to sin in order to be raised to
   new life. The death and resurrection of Jesus has freed
   us from sin and death. We are a new creation, since we
   have died to sin in order to be alive for God in Christ
   Jesus.*

(Year A) Matthew 28:1-10 (Gospel)

   *Mary Magdalene and the other Mary come to the tomb
   on Easter morning. The angel tells the women that Jesus
   has risen from the dead. They inspect the empty tomb
   and are told to tell the disciples. These two women*

bring the good news—Jesus is alive! They have seen him, and the risen Lord offers them peace as the first gift of the new creation.

(Year B) Mark 16:1-8

The Gospel of Mark is known for its simplicity and directness of narration. Mary Magdalene, Mary the mother of James, and Salome go to anoint Jesus. They arrive at the tomb and find the stone rolled back. Once inside, the angel tells them that Jesus the crucified one is now alive and risen from the dead. The women are to tell Peter and the disciples. They flee the tomb in fear and trembling.

(Year C) Luke 24:1-12

The women arrive at the tomb with spices, but the body of Jesus is missing and the stone rolled away. Two men appear with the message that Jesus is not among the dead but the living. The Son of Man had to be crucified, so that on the third day he may rise. The women tell the apostles, but they refuse to believe. Finally Peter runs to the tomb, sees the wrappings, and leaves filled with amazement.

PATIENT WAITING

So much of life is caught up in watching and waiting. There is the waiting that is known by the young, who eagerly anticipate summer vacation, Christmas holidays and graduation. There is the waiting that comes with seeking a first job, working for a promotion, or waiting to see if one passed the bar exam. And, of course, there is the more tension-filled waiting that is known in hospitals and homes, where loved ones struggle for life. There is the joyful expectation of airport waiting, as the son or daughter returns from college. There is the anguished waiting by the phone, experienced by wives and mothers who see loved ones go into the dangerous areas of life. Then there is the ordinary waiting for a bus, a big sports event, or a weekend outing with the family (when it is sure to rain!). Life is waiting, and the way we respond to having to wait reveals much about us. Waiting produces tensions, and in our instant, now society the tensions can test our resolve to be both human and Christian.

Holy Saturday is a day of waiting and watching. Good Friday seemed so final and ultimate: the Cross, the anguish, the death and the stone rolled across the tomb. In this one life, there seemed to be so much promise, love, healing and life. And now it all seems like a bad dream. We are scattered and in hiding. Our hearts are joyless and filled with anxiety. There is no room for love or hope. Only fear occupies us. We have given up so much, and the end seems so bitter and disillusioning. We have given up security, family, home and fishing nets. All we have to show for it is the scandal of the Cross, and a tomb that locks all our hopes in the jaws of death. If only we hadn't been so foolish and followed the teacher. Maybe we can pick up the pieces and carry on. People have a way of forgetting, and becoming preoccupied with other things. It will all blow over soon.

Yet, we cannot dismiss that life so easily. Something still burns within our hearts, and seems to whisper: "Death be not proud," "Death where is your victory and sting?", "He is not among the dead." Why should such words come to us? Once dead, always dead. The cross and the stone have had the last word. Death, the great equalizer, has spoken.

What else are we to do? The Church calls us to be a people of the vigil. We are to watch and wait for the One who told us that he (and we) had to go to Jerusalem and receive a baptism of fire. But he also said that he would rise on the third day. Death would not have the last word in God's world. Life would be stronger than death. In the words of T.S. Eliot, "The ultimate illusion is persistent disillusionment." This vigil calls us to watch and wait for the Crucified One who is also our Risen Lord. The scandal of the Cross joins with the hope of the empty tomb, as the faith of our salvation.

Tonight we watch and wait for the One who bursts the bars of death and proclaims life. Tonight also calls us to look beyond this vigil, and see the Christian life as the vigil that anticipates his coming in glory. We watch and wait for the Easter Jesus, who will establish the fullness of God's Kingdom. Our watching and waiting are not to be done in a passive way. We are to watch with patience, as we labor for the Kingdom. In our everyday lives, we are to do what the women did on that first Easter: go and tell others that Jesus is alive. Go and proclaim the good news that Jesus is not to be found among the dead. Go into the world and preach that the Crucified One is the Risen Lord.

We spend so much of life watching and waiting. We can be disappointed, frustrated and ignored so often. We can grow tired of waiting for the one who does not come. Tonight we watch and wait with eager hearts, with the inner tension that comes with good news. Tonight we shall not be disappointed. The One we wait for is risen. We no longer move among the dead. We go forth in hope with this news: Christ has died, Christ is risen, Christ will come again.

A Time To Be (Re)Born

Throughout these forty days, we have been involved in a journey toward God. These forty days have been an intense search for God. However, all of life is a long search for God, who is beyond yet near at hand. We have also been on a journey or (re)birth and renewal. We have been involved in that most difficult of all human experiences—change. We have been challenged to give up the comfortable and well-traveled road. We have been called to surrender the wisdom of this world, which is really folly to God. Throughout these forty days, we have wandered in the desert of our heart and our everyday life. We have examined the idols and golden calves that clutter our lives and leave no room for the God who alone gives life in abundance.

Lent is often thought of as forty days of negativity, with highlights of all that is bad in the human condition. However, throughout our readings and meditations, we have seen that Lent is really a season of grace and life. It has been a time to pause and consider who or what is the ultimate concern of our life. Lent has been the time for being liberated from all that keeps us from God, and also the time that frees us to be for others as much as we are for ourselves. The old insecurities and uncertainties have been faced and overcome, through the transforming power of the Cross and resurrection.

Throughout our Biblical readings, there has been much talk about conversion, repentance and the need to turn from sin. This is expected during Lent. However, the most unexpected discovery in our Lenten journey is the story of God as unbounded love and fidelity. Yahweh is a God who cares, loves, pursues and gets passionately involved with His people. He is a God who acts with mighty deeds to create, liberate and sustain all who love Him and remain faithful to the covenant. Yahweh does not want our animal sacrifices, ashes, sackcloth or money if our heart is not also given. Yahweh gives Himself completely, and expects that we will do the same. Furthermore, it is never enough to love Yahweh without at the same time loving our neighbor as ourselves. To be a person and a community of justice and concern (for the poor, widowed, orphaned, unborn, sick, elderly, dying and powerless) is to be in covenant with Yahweh.

The depth of God's unbounded love is revealed in Jesus and the Paschal Mystery. God's love and involvement with humanity and history takes an ultimate turn in the Word becoming flesh. Jesus announces to us the year of liberation and grace. The enemies of humankind, sin and death, are not to have the last word. Life is stronger than death, and hope will not be disappointed. The Crucified One is now the Risen Lord, who calls all men and women to be born again. We are now called to live a new way and to experience reality through the symbols of the Cross and the empty tomb.

Lent is the time which reminds us that, apart from Jesus and the community of faith, we can do nothing. To live is to be in relationship to a reality larger than ourselves. To truly live is to be part of the Really Real who spoke at Sinai, and from the Cross, and speaks to us now in the depths of our hearts.

Birth involves pain, tears and the shedding of blood. Yet birth, and all that is involved with it, also speaks of life and hope. Our journey toward God is really a journey which involves our willingness to experience the pain of (re)birth. If we are so willing, we find that the journey is never done in isolation. We join fellow travelers searching for God. The great surprise lies in the realization that God has been searching for us all along. The great mystery is simply that it took us so long to arrive!